John Todhunter

Three Irish Bardic Tales

John Todhunter

Three Irish Bardic Tales

ISBN/EAN: 9783744714495

Printed in Europe, USA, Canada, Australia, Japan

Cover: Foto ©Andreas Hilbeck / pixelio.de

More available books at **www.hansebooks.com**

Three Irish Bardic Tales
Being Metrical Versions of
The Three Tales known
as The Three Sorrows
of Story-Telling

By

John Todhunter

J. M. Dent and Co.,
Aldine House, Gt. Eastern Street, London, E.C.

MDCCCXCVI

PREFACE

Two of the following poems are reprinted from a former volume, the third—'*The Fate of the Sons of Usna*'—now appears for the first time. They are founded upon the three Bardic Tales traditionally known in Ireland as the 'Three Sorrows of Story-Telling.'

In telling again these old stories, I have freely rehandled my materials—not following precisely any one of the many versions of each legend, but appropriating and adopting whatever best suited my purpose in each. Thus, in '*The Fate of the Sons of Usna*,' I have retained the old ending of the tale, which makes Deirdrè live for a year after the death of her lover, a captive in the house of Conchobar; because it seems to me to be an essential part of the primitive legend, and to touch a deeper note of tragedy than that adopted by Joyce in his '*Deirdrè*,' in which she dies upon the grave.

In the original tale of the Sons of Turann, the adventures of Brian and his brothers are told at great length, and I have epitomised them in the form of a Lamentation, not founded on any existing poem.

The lyrical passages in the text are suggested by the lyrics which occur at the more emotional points of the original stories, when the old Story-teller, dropping his prose narrative, says simply: 'And Deirdrè (or some other personage) made this lay.' In many instances, I have paraphrased or adapted these lyrics; but I have not attempted to imitate the complex metrical structure of Irish verse.

A few explanatory notes will be found at the end of the book.

CONTENTS

PAGE

THE DOOM OF THE CHILDREN OF LIR—

THE TUNING OF THE HARP 3

THE FIRST DUAN—THE DOOM OF THE CHILDREN OF LIR . . 7

,, SECOND ,, THE SWANS ON DERRYVARRAGH . . . 13

,, THIRD ,, THE SWANS ON SRUTH-NA-MOYLE . . 18

,, FOURTH ,, THE SWANS IN THE BANNA . . . 24

,, FIFTH ,, THE SWANS IN ERRIS DOMNANN . . 28

,, SIXTH ,, THE COMING OF THE FAITH . . . 36

,, SEVENTH ,, THE SWANS' DELIVERANCE . . . 40

THE FATE OF THE SONS OF USNA—

THE FIRST DUAN—THE COMING OF DEIRDRÈ 47

,, SECOND ,, THE FOSTERING OF DEIRDRÈ . . . 55

,, THIRD ,, THE SONS OF USNA 62

,, FOURTH ,, THE RED KING 72

,, FIFTH ,, THE FLIGHT FROM ALBA 83

PAGE

THE FATE OF THE SONS OF USNA—*continued*—

  . The Sixth Duan—The Pledge of Fergus .   .   .   :   96

    ,,   Seventh ,,   The Red Branch House .   .   .   112

    ,,   Eighth ,,   The Death of the Sons of Usna .   126

    ,,   Ninth ,,   The Death of Deirdrè .   .   .   139

THE LAMENTATION FOR THE THREE SONS OF
    TURANN—

    The Little Lamentation   147

    The First Sorrow   147

    The Second Sorrow   149

    The Great Lamentation   150

    The Death-Song of Turann   157

NOTES   159

THE DOOM
OF THE CHILDREN OF LIR

THE DOOM OF THE CHILDREN OF LIR

THE TUNING OF THE HARP.

I tune the harp for my singing,
I sing the sorrow of Lir,
Sorrowful is my song.

1.

Sad were the wizard race, the Tribe of De Danann,
Sad from the victor swords of Milith's warlike sons,
When, from the last lost fight for lordship of the streams
Of Eri, back they fled, from Tailtin, to their hills.

2.

To the hosting of the chiefs, upon the Daghda's dun,
Together then they drew their war-sick banners pale,
Together drew their hosts, war-wearied and dismayed,
And said: 'Let one be Lord, to the healing of us all!'

3.

Five were the chiefs who rose, with challenge of their deeds
Claiming in lofty words the Over-Kingship there:
Bōv Derg, the Daghda's son; Ilbrac of Assaroe;
And Lir of the White Field in the plain of Eman Macha.

4

And after them stood up Midhir the Proud, who reigned
Upon the hills of Bri, of Bri the loved of Liath,
Bri of the broken heart; and last was Angus Ogue;
All these had many voices, but for Bōv Derg were most.

5.

Then all took sun and moon for their sureties, to obey him,
Bōv Derg, the holy King; save Lir and all his clan.
For Lir withdrew in ire, frowning, and spake no word,
And after him his clan went frowning from the tryst.

6.

And marching from the dun, his war-men at his back,
A thundercloud of wrath, frighting the peaceful day,
He passed to his own place, and sat him down in grief
And anger, many days, brooding upon his wrong.

7.

But those about Bōv Derg were wroth at Lir, and said:
'Give us the word, Bōv Derg, and Lir shall be an heap
Of bleaching bones, cast out and suddenly forgot,
And memory name no more his clan without a cairn.'

8.

'Nay,' said Bōv Derg: 'Not so, Lir is a mighty name,
Greater in war than I, dear as my head to me.
Leave Lir in peace to hold the lordship of his land,
The dragon of our coasts, to daunt Fomorian ships.'

9.

So Lir sat down, unharried, on his hill of the White Field
In anger many days.   Then there went forth a cry
Of wail through all the north, and down the Shannon stream,
A wail in the west, a wail in the south : ' The wife of Lir is dead,
And Lir like winter's frost that melts away in tears ! '

10.

And Bōv Derg heard that cry, and said : ' This woe of Lir
Shall heal our breach ; ' and sent rich gifts to him, and said :
' Behold I have three maidens, fostered in my house,
Of one fair mother borne, fresh as young hawthorn buds,
Sweeter than summer's breath : choose out the fairest now
Oova, or Oifa next, or youngest of them all,
Eva.   Choose thou ; and peace be knit betwixt us twain.'

11.

Good seemed that word to Lir, and he hastened from his hill,
His chariots were three score, their wheels outshone the sun,
His horsemen swift as hawks, splendid as dragonflies
In belted mail.   He rode, and came beside Lough Derg,
There met Bōv Derg, and there abode that day in peace.

12.

That night glad was Bōv Derg, and made, for love of Lir,
A mighty feast, and there, at the High-Queen's right hand,
Lir saw the maidens three, Oova, and Oifa next,
And, youngest of them all, Eva.   ' Choose,' said Bōv Derg :
Lir looked, and sang this lay :

CHOOSING SONG OF LIR.

1.

Three things there be most beautiful
In the softness of their splendour :
The sun in the west, the moon on the water,
And the dawn-star's tremulous light.

2.

Three are the maids before me,
All wonderful in beauty,
Oova, Oifa, Eva,
No man could choose between them.

3.

And now I dare not wrong thee,
Oova, to pass thee over,
First-born shall be first-wed :
Be thou my heart's consoling !

13.

Thereat Bōv Derg praised Lir, that righteous was his choice.
And mighty was the ale-feast at the wedding of that bride ;
For wed they were that night, and morn beheld the splendour
Of the bringing home of Oova, the wife of war-like Lir.

14.

And first a girl and boy she bore at one fair birth,
The sweet-voiced Fianoula, and Oodh with golden hair ;
And next two sons she bore, twins of one fatal hour,
Fiachra and Conn ; and died that hour she heard them cry.

15.

Thus Oova, bearing men, in honoured motherhood
Went piteously to death ; and by the Shannon's stream
A wail went north and south : 'The wife of Lir is dead !
And motherless his babes, cold in the bed of Lir !'

16.

And Bōv Derg heard that wail, and said : 'Ochone for Lir!
Ochone for his young babes, cold is their bed this day !
Thee must he wed, Oifa—mother thy sister's babes.'
And cold went Oifa then to the cold house of Lir.

> *Sorrowful is my song,*
> *The song of the sorrow of Lir,*
> *The harp is tuned for my singing.*

THE FIRST DUAN.

THE DOOM OF THE CHILDREN OF LIR.

> *Sorrowful is my song,*
> *Of songs most sorrowful,*
> *The song of the doom of the Children of Lir.*

I.

So Oifa dwelt with Lir, as mother of his children,
One daughter and three sons, wide was their beauty's fame ;
And Bōv Derg loved them well, and when the daisy's gleam
Silvered the fields of spring, they dwelt with him in joy.

2.

And there Fianoula sang, shaming the blackbird's flute,
And Oodh of the golden hair cast far his boyish spear,
And, leaping like a roe, flew Fiachra o'er the streams,
And Conn, the blue-eyed, roving with his sling, was busy too,

3·

Great was the love of Lir for these, past love of fathers ;
His heart went where they went, and never from their feet,
His feet for long were far, and still his face would turn
After them, east or west, as the daisy's after day.

4·

And when the season fell for their coming home from Bōv,
Glad grew the heart of Lir, as earth's at kiss of spring.
By night he kept them near, and oft ere dawn was grey
Hungry with love he rose, to lie down among his children.

5·

But Oifa in her heart said : ' I am but a nurse
For these my sister's brood : I have no child : and here
Despised I dwell.'   And sick she lay in bitter teen,
Dumb on her bed, a year, nursing her heart's cold snake.

6.

Then pale she rose, and pale she drest in jewelled fire
Her beauty's baleful star, and said : ' Lo, daisied spring
Kindles her emerald torch among the groves of Lir.
Bōv Derg beholds, and dreams of rosy faces nigh.'

7·

She flashed her charms on Lir, and Lir bade yoke the steeds,
And kissed his mounting sons, who laughed to go with her ;
But long Fianoula clung round her grey father's neck,
Weeping to say farewell ; boding some evil doom.

8.

So Oifa took the four, and fiercely driving came
Upon a place of Druids, and said : ' Come, kill me now
This plague with some swift charm ! ' ' Get hence ! ' the Druids
    cried,
' Thou art the plague, Oifa ; fear thou the Druids' curse.'

9.

And on she rode in wrath, and reined beside a wood
Her foaming steeds, and took the children in her hands,
Muttering, to a deep glade ; Fianoula weeping went,
For horror of the way, and boding of her doom.

10.

Then Oifa drew her skeene, and would have slain them there ;
But Conn looked wondering up: 'Mother, what means that knife?'
' Wolves ! ' she cried out: ' Wolves! wolves!'   He whirled his
    tiny sling
And said : ' Lo ! we are here ; no wolf shall do thee harm.'

11. .

And sick with a strange dread, fearing to see their blood,
She cast her skeene away, and led them wondering back,
Muttering : ' The Druids' curse ! I fear the Druids' curse.
I'll crave no charm of theirs, my magic serves as well.'

12.

So they rode on, and came in the hot afternoon
To Derryvarragh Lough ; she stared upon its water,
And said :- ' Go in and bathe ! '   And naked, in delight,
The children shouting ran, and plunged in the cool mere.

13.

Then rose the witch, and muttering paced she upon the shore
A Druid's maze, and raised her witch-wand in her hand,
And smote the children there, and they were seen no more,
But on the lake four Swans beheld their plumes, amazed.

THE WITCH-SONG OF OIFA.

Out, evil brood of Lir,
O'er the waters of your wailing ;
Strange in his ear shall wail your tale
As the dumb cry of a bird.

FIANOULA'S ANSWER.

Witch-mother, thou bale of Lir,
On the waters of our wailing
Thou hast set us without a boat afloat,
In the nakedness of birds !

14.

Then the four Swans swam near, and huddled by the shore
Wept at the feet of Oifa ; Fianoula weeping said :
'O causeless hate that smites us, orphans in thy house,
Whose love smiled in thy face, things easy to be loved!

15.

'Evil thy deed has been, evil shall be thy fate ;
For those whose eyes look now for us, and long must look,
Have magic strong as thine.   They will avenge the Swans ;
Therefore assign some end of the ruin thou hast wrought.'

16.

Fear in the witch's heart was gendering with her hate,
Seeing her evil thought grown to an evil deed,
Yet stern she cried : ' The worse for asking be ye all ! '
And pale with hate she sang the spell-song of their doom :

OIFA'S SONG OF DOOM.

1.

The doom of the Children of Lir,
Thus Oifa dooms them,
Go pine in the feathers of swans
Till the North shall wed the South.

2.

Three hundred years shall ye float
On the stillness of Derryvarragh :
On the tossing of Sruth-na-Moyle,
Unsheltered, three hundred years.

3.

Three hundred years shall ye keene
With the curlews of Erris Domnann ;
Till the bell rings in Inis Glory
I curse you : nine hundred years !

17.

The four Swans heard their doom, and huddled by the shore
Wept at the feet of Oifa.   Fianoula weeping said :
' This is a mighty curse, O mother of our tears !
Unmothered, comfortless, cold through the age-long night ! '

FIANOULA'S PRAYER.

A boon, a boon, O mother,
For the sorrowful Children of Lir !
Sad is the voice of children
In the terrors of the night.·

18.

Fear in the witch's heart was gendering with her hate,
Seeing her evil thought grown to an evil deed;
And on her tongue was laid a spell more strong than hers,
In fear, not ruth, she spake this lightening of their doom:

OIFA'S ANSWER.

1.

A boon, a boon I yield you,
Ye sorrowful Children of Lir!
Man's reason shall breed within you
Sweet words in the tongue of men.

2.

Sweet, sweet be your voices,
Ye mournful Swans of Lir!
The sad, sweet moan of your music
Shall comfort the sick with sleep.

3.

Sweet, sweet be your voices,
Ye sorrowful Swans of Lir!
Your song from the seas of Eri
Shall comfort the sorrows of men.

4.

Sweet, sweet be your voices,
Ye magical Swans of Lir!
A nation's desolation
Shall witch the world in your song.

19.

Then from the Swans went Oifa, and hasting from the shore
Fled from her triumph, pale, hate glutted; and the Swans,
Banished from hopes of men, and comfort of their kind
Swam in a knot forlorn into the clouds of doom.

*This was the doom of the Children of Lir
Of dooms most doleful,
Sorrowful is my song.*

THE SECOND DUAN.

THE SWANS ON DERRYVARRAGH.

*Sorrowful is my song
Of songs most sorrowful,
The song of the doom of the Children of Lir.*

1.

So from the Swans went Oifa, and cold slept in her heart
Revenge's glutted snake; and to Bōv Derg she came.
Bōv Derg her coming marked, and starting from his place
Asked her: 'Where are the children?' She softly smiling, said:

2.

'Strange madness works in Lir: his brow grew black in wrath
When hither I would come. He loves not thee nor me.
No more his flock may rove out of his jealous eye,
Come to thee never more. I am weary, and would rest.'

3.

Thereat amazed, Bōv Derg laid ambush in his mind,
Marking the witch's eye that glittered like a snake's
With inward fire, and felt a lurking evil there;
And sent to Lir, seeking the children in their home.

4.

Lir, when he heard, his wrath flaming from sudden dread,
Took horse for the hill of Bōv, with visions by the way
Of Oifa's murderous mind ; and schemed some vast revenge,
Rushing in flames of wrath by Derryvarragh Lough.

5.

The Swans beheld afar, and with a human wail
Of song over the water, called on the name of Lir.
Pierced with their wistful sad melodious moan, sat Lir
Fumbling his rein, aghast, as wailing they drew nigh.

THE SONG OF THE SWANS.

Tarry, Lir, and hear
The song of the Swans !
Pity thy children, Lir,
The Swans forlorn, thy children !

6.

Hearing that cry, ran Lir all trembling to the shore,
And bent in ruth to kiss the piteous feathery things
That from the water wailed, and on the weeping Swans
Full fast, in loving ruth, hot fell the tears of Lir !

7.

And well each child he knew, sewn in its feathery shroud.
And stroked with passionate hand Oodh's o'er-snowed golden head,
And stroked Fianoula's neck, writhing to meet his touch,
And stroked his Fiachra's wings, and the downy crest of Conn.

8.

Then burst in sobs his voice : ' Oh, beggared in one day !
Whence are these swans for children ? Whence falls this feathery
    blight :
This wrong unbearable, that vengeance cannot cure ?
Oifa, is this thy deed ? ' Fianoula answered low :

SONG OF FIANOULA.

1.

Hot are thy tears, O Lir,
On the feathers of the Swans ;
But cold shall rain the rains
Long ages upon thy children.

2.

Thou gavest us, O Lir,
A cruel witch for our mother !
Poor father ! for thee I weep
She has given thee Swans for children.

3.

Three hundred years must we tread
Lake-water in Derryvarragh :
On the saltness of Sruth-na-Moyle
Must welter, three hundred years.

4.

Three hundred years must we cleave
The billows of Erris Domnann:
Till the bell rings in Inis Glory
She cursed us—nine hundred years!

9.

Great was the lamentation and the love between them there;
Loud was the Swans' lament, and loud the grief of Lir;
And with his children four he there lay down that night,
With the Swans he made his bed by the shores of Derryvarragh.

10.

But when the dawn grew bright he hastened on his way
To the house of the High-King. Oifa before Bōv Derg
Was called, and to her face Lir told his piteous tale.
Wearily still she smiled: 'I have done it—let me die!'

11.

Stern rose Bōv Derg in wrath: 'I lay my druid spell
On thy confessing tongue, to answer what vile shape
Is most abhorred by thee?' She writhed, compelled with pain,
Crying with a ghastly shriek: 'A demon of the air!'

12.

'Take then that shape,' he said, and smote her with his wand;
And her blue eyes grew white as dazzling leprosy,
Her hideous body seemed the snake-fiend of her heart
Burst forth on dragon wings. And Bōv Derg spoke her doom:

THE DOOM OF OIFA.

1.

From the tribes of men fly Oifa,
Pale outlaw of the air,
Till the wind shall cease to wail
For Eri and her woes!

2.

Go howl on the blast, howl Oifa
O'er the land where the Banshee cries :
In the shade of thy dragon wings
Fall horror of brooding fate.

3.

Abhorred of men, howl Oifa
O'er the mountains of Inisfail :
The Swans of Lir shall have comfort
Long ere thy end of woes.

13.

So howling on the blast fled from the face of men
Oifa, for evermore.   But Bōv Derg went with Lir
Back to the gentle Swans, for solace of their song ;
And with them by the lake they dwelt three hundred years.

14.

And there dwelt peace : there came, by septs, the De Danann,
There Milith's warlike sons sat down with them in peace ;
For all men loved the Swans, for comfort of their song.
And peace with all her arts reigned there three hundred years.

15.

Then said Fianoula : ' Ah, sweet brothers, know ye not
Our age is ended here ?   To-night our flight must be.'
Then sorrow for their fate fell on the sons of Lir,
' We were still men,' they said, ' here dwelling with our kin.'

B

FLITTING-SONG OF THE SWANS.

1.

Our beautiful feathers
Must we drench in salt surges,
No night brine-unbittered
For the Children of Lir!

2.

Farewell, Derryvarragh,
Farewell, friendly faces,
To the gulls and the curlews
Fly the Children of Lir.

16.

Loud was the Swans' lament, and loud the grief of Lir,
And long the lamentation and the love between them there.
Then the four Swans soared high, and swiftly to the north
Flew from the eyes of Lir, and lit on Sruth-na-Moyle.

This is the song of the flitting of the Swans,
Of songs most mournful,
Sorrowful is my song!

THE THIRD DUAN.

THE SWANS ON SRUTH-NA-MOYLE.

Sorrowful is my song,
Of songs most sorrowful,
The song of the doom of the Children of Lir.

1.

Now sang the shrill sea-wind through the feathers of the Swans,
And cold round their white breasts the brine of Sruth-na-Moyle
Boiled in the bitter surge; and bitter was their lot,
Tossing unsheltered on the tides of Sruth-na-Moyle.

2.

And once, ere sunset, fell a darkness on the deep,
And sharp Fianoula cried : ' Ochone for us this night !
Bad is our preparation ! the storm is in our wings
To drive us four apart on seas unknown to-night.

3.

' Forlorn this night shall be our bed in the black waters,
Forlorn our lonely sailing on seas without a star ;
Sharing in love no more the comfort of our wings,
Sad must we walk to-night the waves of Sruth-na-Moyle !

4.

' Tell me then, where shall be the trysting of the Swans,
If life be left in us to see the storm go down ? '
' Be it the Rock of the Seals, Carrig-na-Rōn,' they cried,
' Carrig-na-Rōn's the word !   May we all see it soon ! '

5.

Ere midnight swooped the storm, and scowling o'er the deep
They saw the eyes of Oifa, and heard her in the blast
Howling, as they were driven apart on the wild sea.
None knew his brother's path all night, nor saw his own.

6.

For all night long the storm dashed them about the deep
In sleet and freezing spray, blind ; and the lightning's glare
Showed them but heaving mountains, black on the gleaming sea ;
So all night long they fought for life with the rude waves.

7.

With night fled the fierce wind.   They knew the east, and steered
O'er seas of separation, while rosily in the dawn
Gleamed their subsiding crests.   But the four were far apart,
And lonely came Fianoula first to the Rock of Seals.

8.

To the rock she fluttered ; there, with wings too weak for flight,
Stared on the waste of waters thundering about her feet ;
And many a foamy crest, white on the lowering grey,
Her anxious eyes believed a swan—that never came.

FIANOULA'S LAMENTATION ON THE ROCK.

1.

Bad is life in my state,
My wings droop at my sides,
The furious blast hath shattered
The heart in my breast for Oodh.

2.

Three hundred years as a swan
On the waters of Derryvarragh
I was shut from my human shape ;
But worse is one night like this

3.

Belov'd the three, oh, belov'd the three
Who nestled beneath my wings !
Till the dead come to meet the living
I shall meet them never more.

4.

No sign of Oodh nor Fiachra
Of Conn the comely no news !
Have pity for me who live, ye dead,
In misery bad is life !

9.

There sat she till night fell, and through that night forlorn,
Till the rising of the day, blind with her dazzling watch.
At last there came a swan—young Conn, with drooping head
And feathers drenched in brine.   Then joy sang in her heart.

10.

And Conn she comforted beneath her wings, that glowed
With the new glow of her heart ; and then came Fiachra, cold,
Half dead, a drifting waif ; and word he could not speak,
For hardship of the sea.   Him too she cheered with life.

11.

The third long night the three together on the rock
Nestled, and sighed for Oodh.   And, with the rising sun,
Came Oodh, his glorious head high-held, his feathers preened,
And flew to them, and brought the sun upon his wings.

12.

Warm on the Swans the sun shone, and a rush of joy
Startled the tide of life in sad Fianoula's breast ;
And heartily the three welcomed their missing one,
Heartily hailed they all their brother from the deep.

13.

And Oodh Fianoula warmed with the feathers of her breast ;
And over Fiachra spread her right wing ; and her left,
The wing of her heart, o'er Conn.   ' Bitter these days,' she said,
' But worse will come to pinch the wandering Swans of Lir.'

14.

There dwelt they, with the seals, the human-hearted seals,
That loved the Swans, and far followed with sad soft eyes,
Doglike, in sleek brown troops, their singing, o'er the sea;
So for their music yearned the nations of the seals.

15.

And there they sorely learned the hardship of the sea,
The misery of the birds, their penury and toil.
Summer passed, winter came, and nipt them with a night
The like of which, for cold, they had never felt before.

16.

That January night upon the rock they lay,
One heap of feathery snow, their inmost feathers cold
As fleeces filled with frost.   One huddling heap they lay
Cold in the windy tent of their sun-loving wings.

17.

Hoarse o'er the hissing waves howled Oifa in the blast,
And dreadful through the night the chill glare of her eyes
Gleamed in the dazzling snow; and through the Swans the surf
Shot arrows, burning cold, barbed by the stinging frost.

18.

Thus they endured that night, close-huddled to keep warm
Life's embers in them.   There late morning found them, all
Fast frozen to their bed.   They roused their ebbing powers,
And grimly, with wild pain, at length tore themselves free.

19.

But on the frozen rock their bed was flaked with blood,
Bent quills, and bloody down, and broken plumes; for there
They left the skin of their breasts, they left the skin of their feet,
And half the soaring strength of their sun-loving wings.

FIANOULA'S LAMENTATION IN THE COLD.

1.

Ochone for the Swans left bare
Of the warm fleece of their feathers !
Ochone for the feet that bleed
On the rough teeth of the rocks !

2.

False, false was our mother,
When she drove us with Druid's craft
Adrift on the roaring waters,
In the outlawry of birds.

3.

For happy home she gave us
The fleeting surge of the sea,
For share of the lordly ale-feast
The loathing of bitter brine.

4.

One daughter, and three sons,
Behold us, Lir, on the rocks,
Featherless, comfortless, cold,
We print our steps in blood.

20.

Then, with their bleeding wounds, they plunged in Sruth-na-Moyle,
For painful was their path on the limpet-studded rocks.
There on the wandering tides they made their patient bed,
Until their wounds were whole, their wings bold on the blast.

This is the song of the hardship of the Swans,
Of songs most mournful,
Sorrowful is my song.

THE FOURTH DUAN.

THE SWANS IN THE BANNA.

Sorrowful is my song,
Of songs most sorrowful,
The song of the doom of the Children of Lir.

1.

Then day by day, the Swans, new winged, in sounding strength
Far-soaring, north and south, twixt Erin and Albain,
Would visit in his isle their brother Manannan,
Grey wizard of the sea; much solace found they there.

2.

Wizard to wizard, oft, Time in his cloudy cave
He met; and he could spell some rune of things to come.
And in Fianoula's ear his mild prophetic word
Breathed shell-like thunders dim from coming tides of death.

3.

But ever to the rock the Swans flew back at night,
As was their doom.   And well the happy coasts they knew,
Barred from their landing ; where in sunny bays full oft
They wept in the murmuring wind, sad for its inland voice.

4.

And once when they had sailed from the unresting sea
Far up, by Banna's mouth, to the green heart of the hills,
They saw a moving light gleam snakelike down a vale,
Mocking the sun for splendour, greatening as they gazed.

5.

And Conn cried : ' Lo where shine the Faery Chivalry,
Like dragons of the sun !   White are their steeds, and there
March Milith's warlike sons, and borne aloft I see
Banners, wherein we live blazoned—the Swans of Lir ! '

6.

Great joy was there, forsooth, when the Swans met their kin,
The stalwart sons of Bōv : one band Oodh Sharpwit led,
Fergus the Wizard, one ; and breast-deep in the sea
They plunged to greet the Swans, sought for a hundred years.

7.

And at their kiss the Swans trembled and wept for joy,
Asking a thousand things, dreading some tale of change :
' How goes it with Bōv Derg, and with our father Lir ?
Rest still those veteran oaks in peace upon their hills ? '

8.

Answered the sons of Bōv : 'Gently the snows of time
Sink on the head of Lir, and on the head of Bōv.
Together in Lir's house they keep the Feast of Age,
Merrily as they may, remembering still your song.

9.

'How fare ye in the sea?'   Fianoula sighing said :
' Not to be told our life, for misery, not to be told !
Nor to be told our penury with the toiling tribes of birds !
We in whose train should wait the shining sons of kings !

10.

'For beds of down, long years our breasts rub down the rock,
For honey-coloured mead we drink the hissing surge ;
Happy this night lie down the well-clad thralls of Lir,
But cold in a cold house the children of their king !'

11.

Then sundered from their friends, the Swans to their cold sea
Swam back in sorrow.   Back rode, sundered from the Swans,
The Faery Chivalry, and told their tale to Lir ;
And Lir for love and ruth shed softly tears of age.

12.

'They live?' he sighed, ''tis good !' and pledged with Bōv,
      the Swans.
'What can we do?' they said.   'We cannot change their doom.'
Then o'er their chess once more their hoary age they bent,
And lone flew back the Swans to their lair in Sruth-na-Moyle.

13.

Thus did the Swans fly back to bide in Sruth-na-Moyle
Their full three hundred years; suffering with gulls and terns
The hardship of the sea, they bode three hundred years.
Then said Fianoula : ' Swans, your flitting-time is come.'

FLITTING-SONG OF THE SWANS.

1.

Ochone for our dreary flitting !
Woe to us wandering away
From the coasts and bays that have sheltered
Our sorrows three hundred years !

2.

To the world's end in western Erris,
Ochone for our dreary flitting !
The warmth of our wings must comfort
The bleak wild wind of the west.

3.

Far, far we fly from thy soothing,
Manannàn, thou soft sooth-sayer,
Ochone for our dreary flitting,
To the sea without a shore !

4.

Out of the world, ay, out of the world
The curse of a witch outcasts us,
Shelterless, friendless, nameless,
Ochone for our dreary flitting !

14.

Sore was the Swans' lament, and deep sighed Manannàn,
Sweet was the lamentation, and the love between them there.
Then the four Swans soared high, and swiftly to the west
Flew from the wizard's eye, and lit in the vast sea.

This is the song of the loneliness of the Swans,
Of songs most mournful,
Sorrowful is my song !

THE FIFTH DUAN.

THE SWANS IN ERRIS DOMNANN.

Sorrowful is my song,
Of songs most sorrowful
The song of the doom of the Children of Lir !

1.

By Erris Domnann's cliffs they dwelt.   There first they knew
The ocean without shore ; and in their ears all night
Boomed on with solemn sound the thunder of its waves.
And answering to that sound, their minds were changed for awe.

2.

There, day on boundless day, wonders were in their eye,
Wonders of the great deep.   Blue rolled the unresting waves
And white the boiling surge smote the unflinching rocks.
And, answering to that sight, their minds grew great in awe.

3.

But want they felt, and cold ; and pity wrung their breast
For the sea-faring tribes.   And many a dreadful storm
Smote them, the wrath whereof they had never felt before,
Seeking in land-locked bays what shelter they might win.

4.

But once, when glowing noon slept on the murmuring waves
And the brown basking rocks, an odorous inland breeze
Wafted them o'er the sea faint pulsings of a harp,
Lamenting tones where lived memories of their own dead songs.

5.

Then wondering rose the Swans, and sought on sounding wing
That echo of their woes.   And there, upon the rocks,
They found a harper, grey, with wistful eyes.   His harp
Fell as he cried : ' At last !   Are these the Swans of Lir ? '

6.

They questioned of his name.   ' Ævric,' he said, ' grown grey
Seeking the Swans.   Your tale saddened my dreaming youth,
Waifs of your song, like pools by some forgotten stream
Left lonely on the hills, haunt still this land of sighs.

7.

' I drank, and thirsted still, and am become a cloud
Wandering the world to seek the fountains of the dew.
Oh, fill my thirsting soul with music !   Swans I have loved,
Slay me not with your sight, unsolaced by your song ! '

8.

Wan was his face, o'erflowed by the rivers of his eyes,
And pale the pleading hands stretched to them o'er the sea.
Then the four Swans swam near, and Ævric in the brine
Plunged in, breast-deep, to touch the feathers of the four.

9.

Sweet was their salutation ; and soon between them there
Kindled a mighty love, not soon to cease ; for there
Ævric abode, and long shared with the Swans his food,
And from his hand once more they knew the taste of bread.

10.

Sweet were the songs they taught him, and made him with their lore
First bard of all his time.   Then, feeling death draw near,
He said : ' My time is come : hence must I, and sing your songs
In youthful ears, to keep the heart of Eri green.'

11.

Sorrowing he went ; through tears their eyes looked after him :
Desolate stood his hut, a spectre on the rocks,
Cold as the tomb wherein their happy days lay dead ;
And yet they loved the spot where they had lost a friend.

12.

But Ævric made the heart of Eri bud with song,
Dying when he had made the story of the Swans ;
While for a hundred years the Swans in the great sea
By Erris Domnann bode, in hardships ever new.

13.

Then came a winter night, the like of which for frost
They had never felt before.   Breathless above the sea
The frozen air stood still : its billows hushed in awe,
Freezing without a sound, still stood the mighty deep.

14.

There, beautiful in heaven, throned in her splendour, Night,
An awful presence, dwelt.   Awfully on the sea
The moon looked silent down.   Cold through the icy air
Awfully flamed the stars, alive with deadly light.

15.

Silent, remorseless, swift, blurring the torpid surge,
The flag of ice advanced ; dense round the moving Swans
The thin sea-water grew ; meshed in its creeping net
They moved no more.   ' Death spurs his fated hour,' said Conn.

16.

' Nay, see,' Fianoula said, ' still is the frozen air—
That stillness guards our life.   Howled Oifa on the blast,
The wind's keen fangs to-night had nipt our hearts indeed.
But stark she crouches, cowed by heaven's frosty eyes.'

FIANOULA'S SONG IN THE FROZEN SEA.

1.

Oh ! who shall comfort the Swans ?
The sea, the sea hath betrayed us !
The frost's white wand on thy waters,
We perish by thee, O Sea !

2.

For the freedom of the waves
Brisk, buoyant under our bodies,
Pent here in thy crystal prison,
We pine to be free, O Sea!

3. ·

Great art Thou, God of heaven!
In the trance of the wind and the waters
Thy love walks o'er the sea,
This night is Thy shield reveal'd.

4.

Dread Framer of earth and heaven,
Chastise the strong till they pity,
Give ease to Thy suffering tribes,
Our souls be set free, by Thee!

17.

'Brothers,' she cried, 'believe in the great God of heaven!'
'We do believe,' they said; and straightway on their hearts
Fell peace; and fear was quelled by awe; and a new song
Grew on their golden tongues, hymning the God of heaven:

THE SWANS' SONG OF PRAISE.

FIANOULA.

Great is the God of heaven!

THE THREE BROTHERS.

And wonderful His works!

FIANOULA.

Great is the God of heaven!

THE THREE BROTHERS.

And greatly to be praised!

FIANOULA AND OODH.

In the glorious lights of heaven
His eyes behold our weakness.

FIACHRA AND CONN.

He hath paven the sea with crystal
For the footsteps of His love.

THE FOUR SWANS.

O God, most mighty,
We praise thee out of the waters!
O King of Consolation,
Thy wings are over all!

18.

Even as they sang, the north, far o'er the crystal sea
Budded with phantom fire.   Pale flames, and rays of gloom,
Streamed to the zenith flickering ; and dying, quickening still,
Made, as the low moon dipt, all heaven one throbbing rose.

19.

Fianoula saw, and cried : ‘Terrible saints advance
To the purging of the earth : to the conquering of the nations
Terrible kings advance! Ghostlike our banners flee
To the wan fairy fields.   Oh! where is Lir to-night?’

20.

With morning came the sun and the warm wind of the west,
And split the groaning ice.   Free swam the Swans once more,
Unharmed, on the brisk tide, and on their clanging wings
Soared o'er the churning ice, to their own sheltering bay.

21.

So from that day they dwelt, free in their ocean home,
Knowing both heat and cold; but in hardship or in ease
Over them like a tent was spread the peace of God.
And there they dwelt in peace for still one hundred years.

22.

Then said Fianoula: ' Come, our cruel mother's curse
Withers upon the waters and on the fields of air,
And we are free to fly home to the halls of Lir.
How fares it with our father—does he still see the sun ? '

23.

So the four Swans soared high, and swiftly to the east,
Under the eyes of dawn, flew home to the halls of Lir,
And found them but a heap, and desolation there
Dwelt, and a tongueless grief, as of a harp unstrung.

24.

Sadly his children four by Lir's forgotten hearth
In silence sat them down ; and memories in dim troop,
Orphans of days long dead, stole from their weedy lair
To gaze with wistful eyes upon the orphans four.

THE SWANS' LAMENT FOR THE DESOLATION OF LIR.

1.

A lost dream to us now is our home
Ullagone!   Ochone-a-rie !
Gall to our heart !   Oh, gall to our heart !
Ullagone!   Ochone-a-rie !

2.

A hearthless home, without fire, without joy,
Without a harp, without a hound !
No talk, no laughter, no sound of song,
Ullagone for the halls of Lir !

3.

Where now are the prosperous kings ?
Where are the women ?   Where is the love ?
The kiss of welcome warm on our cheeks ?
The loving tongue of hounds on our hands ?

4.

Oh ! the greatness of our mishap !
Oh ! the length of our evil day !
Bitter to toss between sea and sea,
But worse the taste of a loveless home.

5.

Children we left it, swans we return.
To a strange place, strangers.   None lives to say :
' These are the Children of Lir.'   A dream,
In a dream forgotten are we this night !

6.

Is this the place of music we knew,
Where howls the wolf through the halls of Lir ?
Where mirth in the drinking-horn was born,
Chill falls the rain on the hearth of Lir.

7.

Ullagone !   Ochone-a-rie !
Gall to our hearts is that sight to-night
Ullagone !   Ochone-a-rie !
A lost dream to us now is our home !

25.

So sang they. 'Let us go,' Fianoula said, 'for here
We have no more a home ; back to the breezy west
Our flight must be. Now Lir, wandering in Fairyland,
Beholds a phantom sun.' So spake she, and back they flew.

This is the song of the desolation of Lir,
Of songs most mournful,
Sorrowful is my song !

THE SIXTH DUAN.

THE COMING OF THE FAITH.

A changing song is my song,
Of songs most wondrous,
The song of the doom of the Children of Lir.

1.

So did the Swans fly back from the ruined halls of Lir
To the wild western sea, and, veering southward, came
To Inis Glory of Brendan ; and there they made their home,
Waiting in patient peace the coming of the Faith.

2.

And all the tribes of birds were gathered to them there,
And with sweet fairy singing there in the Lake of Birds
They taught the airy tribes, and comforted their woes ;
Till, as the seals, they loved the singing of the Swans.

3.

Far was their flight by day; along the wild west coast
They roamed to feed, as far as Achill, and at night
Flew back to Inis Glory; and wheresoe'er they moved
Thick waved the following wings of loving flocks of birds.

4.

And there they dwelt in peace till the coming of the Faith,
Till holy Patrick's feet blest Erin's faithless fields;
And then to Inis Glory a priest came, sent of God,
He dreamed not for what end, but came there sent of God.

5.

That priest was Mocholm Ogue; and sorrowful of heart
He came to Inis Glory, and there six days he toiled,
No man to help, and built, serving the Lord, a church;
And resting the seventh day, he hallowed it to Christ.

6.

Marvellous was his work; for great strength in his hands
God put; and there by night, no shelter for his head,
But sheltering as he might the Church's holy things,
He laid him down to sleep, wet with the rain and the dew.

7.

And like the birds he lived, no better than the birds.
Toiling, yet keeping still matins, and nones, and primes.
Then by God's finished house he built himself a hut,
Where like the birds he lived, no better than the birds.

8.

Yet heavy was his mood ; questioning God he thought :
' Why am I wasted, thus ; from the world's throbbing heart
Aloof, in peaceless peace, God's battles at my back ?
Shall I feed the fish with praise, birds with the bread of God ? '

9.

But steadfast in his deeds, not scanting prayer nor praise,
He toiled ; and the seventh day, in blessed bread and wine,
Christ came to win the West.   That grace the sacring bell
To wondering land and sea proclaimed with silver sound.

10.

The sad Swans heard, far, faint, from some dim alien world,
The bell's mysterious tone ; and on the brothers three
Strange terror fell, and wild they dashed through the clear waves,
Till, at Fianoula's call, they waited on her word.

11.

' What ails you thus to fly ? ' she said.   ' What have ye heard ? '
And they : ' We know not what—a faint and fearful voice
Thrills in the shuddering air ! '   ' That is God's bell,' said she,
' The bell that brings us ease.   Blest be the name of God ! '

FIANOULA'S SONG OF DELIVERANCE.

1.

Hark to the Cleric's bell,
Ye sorrowful Swans of Lir !
Give thanks to God for its voice
Calling your souls to rest.

2.

Lift up your hearts in gladness,
Ye sorrowful Swans of Lir!
On the wings of the wind your wings
Lift up to the gates of heaven!

3.

Hark to the Cleric's bell,
Ye comely Children of Lir!
Redeemed from the scorn of tempests,
And the fury of the rocks.

4.

Redeemed from the terror of life,
And icy deserts of death,
Redeemed from earth's enchantment,
Turn to the Cleric's bell!

12.

Then on their sounding wings the Swans their latest flight
Took from the unresting sea, to find the rest of God;
And on the Lake of Birds they lit, and through the night
Praised with sweet fairy music the great God of heaven.

13.

Afar heard Mocholm Ogue the singing of the Swans,
And trembled for strange awe, and wondering prayed that God
Would show him what wild things those were that praised His name.
And it was shown him straight: 'These are the Swans of Lir.'

14.

Then glad was Mocholm Ogue, and penitential tears
Wept before God, and cried: 'A sinful man, O Lord!
Not worthy of this grace, am I, that unto me
Thou hast sent these prisoned souls to loose from their long woe.'

15.

With dawn he rose, and ran, and standing by the lake,
Called through the mists of morn : ' Are ye the Swans of Lir ? '
The Swans heard him, and came, and wept beside the shore :
' Waiting release we live, the charmed Children of Lir.'

16.

' Blessed be God ! ' said he.   ' For this God sent me hither,
To save you out of sin.   Put all your trust in God.'
He kissed the weeping Swans, and took them to his place,
And there they dwelt with him, four weary things at rest.

17.

Hearing the mass they dwelt, and there with Mocholm Ogue
Kept the canonical hours.   And great content and joy
The Cleric had of them, his heart soared at their song ;
And trouble dashed no more the spirit of the Swans.

This is the song of the coming of the Faith,
Of songs most wondrous,
A changed song is my song.

THE SEVENTH DUAN.

THE SWANS' DELIVERANCE.

Wonderful is my song,
Of songs most wonderful,
The song of the peace of the Children of Lir.

1.

There to that isle of peace, in the world's dark seas of woe,
As birds flock to be fed, the heathen of the wilds
Flocked at the Cleric's bell, wondering to hear the Swans ;
And barbarous hearts were turned to Christ in that fair spot.

2.

Then said the Cleric : ' Swans, ye are made the birds of Christ,
'Tis meet ye bear His yoke.'   Fair silver chains he wrought,
And chained them, two and two, Fianoula paired with Oodh,
Fiachra with Conn.   And ease it seemed that yoke to bear.

3.

But now was come the day of their accomplished doom,
When the North should wed the South ; for Lairgnen, Colman's son,
The King of Connaught, took the daughter of a King,
Finghin of Munster's child, Deoch, to be his wife.

4.

Soon Deoch heard the fame of the magic singing Swans,
And envy gnawed her heart to have them for her own.
No peace could Lairgnen find, putting her off with words ;
For fierce was her desire to make their fame her own.

5.

' Art thou a king,' she said, ' and dar'st not take these birds
To give me my desire ?   Empty shall be thy bed,
Empty thy house of me until I have the Swans.
Seek me to-night, and cold the comfort thou shalt find.'

6.

Ere night, in sooth, she fled, seeking her father's dun ;
But Lairgnen followed her, hot on her fiery track,
Caught her at Kill Dalua, and swearing by the Swans
That she should have her will, brought her, still sullen, home.

7.

Then the king sent in haste a kerne to Mocholm Ogue,
Asking him for the Swans; but soon with empty hands
The messenger came back.   And Deoch laughed in scorn,
And hot grew Lairgnen's cheek at the taunting of her eyes.

8.

In sudden wrath he rose, and caught her by the wrist,
Crying: 'To horse, woman, and thou shalt have the birds!'
So forth in haste they flung, and all on fire they rode
To Inis Glory, and there drew rein before the church.

9.

In the door stood Mocholm Ogue, and Lairgnen, loud in wrath,
Cried to him: 'Is this true, thou hast refused the Swans?'
But calm the Cleric spoke: 'These are the birds of God.
Kneel thou before His cross, for pardon and for peace.'

10.

But Lairgnen, pushing by, strode to the altar straight,
And seized the shuddering Swans, and by their silver chains,
A pair in either hand, he dragged them from the church,
Crying, with a fierce laugh: 'Here, woman, take thy birds!'

11.

But lo! a wondrous thing: suddenly from the Swans
Slack fell their feathery coats, and there once more they stood,
Children; yet weird with age, weird with nine hundred years
Of woe: four wistful ghosts from childhood's daisied field.

12.

Four children there they stood, naked as when in glee
They plunged into the lough. And Mocholm Ogue in haste
Clad them in spotless fair white robes of choristers.
But Lairgnen curst he loud, with Deoch, for their sin.

13.

Then, curst by Mocholm Ogue, curst with the curse of God,
Fled Lairgnen from that spot, with Deoch, curst of God :
And in their ears that curse on the white lips of fear
Muttered for ever, till their lives had fearful end.

14.

But sad was Mocholm Ogue, for his dear comrades the Swans ;
' And sad,' Fianoula said, ' this day for us and thee.
Our parting hour is come, when death must give us peace,
Haste with the water now that makes us one with Christ!

15.

' And Cleric, chaste and dear, friend of our faltering hopes,
Gate of our glory, pray for our sinful passing souls,
And give us, of thy love, God's oil upon our heads,
God's bread between our lips, that we may win thy heaven.'

FIANOULA'S DEATH-SONG.

1.

A grave, a grave is my craving,
And the reach of my desire :
A grave for the Children of Lir—
Long suffered, long loved the Children !

2.

Together we lived, together
Shall hold us, hoping for heaven,
One sister and three brothers,
The grave of the Children of Lir !

3.

Thus, friend, shalt thou lay us,
One sister and three brothers,
At my right hand Fiachra, and Conn by my heart,
And Oodh, Oodh, in my bosom.

4.

Great was thy love unto us,
O father of our souls !
And great the love thou wilt bury
In the grave of the Children of Lir !

16.

Then were the four baptised, and with the blessed host
Comforted.　Houseled then the first time and the last,
And praising God, that night they sang their souls away,
In the sure hope of heaven.　But sad was Mocholm Ogue.

17.

And in one grave he laid, keeping Fianoula's word,
The four Children of Lir ; and masses for their souls
He said, and wrote their names in Ogham on their stone ;
And in the church he hung the four white shapes of swans.

Sung is the song of the Children of Lir,
Of songs most wonderful :
Wonderful is my song !

THE FATE
OF THE SONS OF USNA

THE FATE OF THE SONS OF USNA

THE FIRST DUAN.

THE COMING OF DEIRDRÈ.

A feast was in the house of Felimy Mac Dal,
Chief Bard of Conchobar; and, bidden of the Bard,
There feasted with his chiefs, flower of the great Red-Branch,
Conchobar the High-King, of Rury's blood, who reigned
O'er Ulster and the North, in Eman of the Kings.

There in the Bard's high house loud was the revelry,
Keen was the cry of harps, glorious the war of song,
When singers old in fame with taunt and challenge met,
And golden voice with voice, contending for men's praise,
Chanted, in sounding words that rang like brazen strokes,
Great Champions' deeds and deaths, Bard answering to Bard.

No dearth was found that night, in Eman of the Kings,
Of Bards, or Shanachies, or Druids; for the court
Of Conchobar was famed for Bards and bardic lore;
And ancient learning none loved better, of all Kings
That e'er in Ireland wore the *cath-barr* of a King.

47

From the King's board each day fed Felimy Mac Dal,
Who bare a golden Branch of Music in his hand,
As royal Bard, and ruled o'er famous Bards a score,
Who bare Branches of silver; and four-score Bards and ten,
Well-skilled in song, who bare Branches of bronze.   Each one
Could with his Bell-branch lull the angry heart asleep.

So Kings and Chiefs and Bards, in Eman of the Kings,
Feasted with Felimy; and rank and order due
Were kept between them all, each Bard, or Chief, or King
Being marshalled to his place by stewards of the feast.
But Conchobar alone came armed into the hall.

And there the amber mead, crowning the golden cup,
Welcomed each noble guest.   There Conall Carnach sat,
Whose eyes, renowned in song, the blue eye and the brown,
Abashed his foes; but now beamed kindly as he pledged
The man of glorious heart who laughed a realm away,
Fergus Mac Roy; who now pledged him again, and laughed,
With frank heart-easing roar, the laugh that all men loved.

So Fergus laughed, and looked a mighty man of men;
Ruddy his face, and red the great beard on his breast,
Fergus, whose heart contained the laughter and the tears
Of all the world; who held the freedom of his mood,
Love, and the dreaming harp that made the world a dream,
The comradeship of feasts, the wild joy of the chase,
Dearer than power; Fergus, who sang in after years
The raid of red Queen Meave, the wasting of the Branch,
Breaches in famous loves, long wars, and deaths renowned
Of many a feaster there; where Conall now in mirth
Pledged his old friend, whose son ere long by him should fall.

And there Fardia felt the broad hand of his death
Laid on his shoulder now in comrade's love ; for there,
A friend beside his friend, unarmed Cuchullin sat,
Like a swift hound for strength and graceful slenderness,
In the first flower of his youth ; the colours of his face
Fresh as the dawning day, and in his clear blue eyes
The glad undaunted light of life's unsullied morn.

There in his royal state, a grave man among Kings,
Sat Conchobar, still, stern.   The dark flame of his face
Tamed, as the sun the stars, all faces else : a face
Of subtle splendour ; brows of wisdom, broad and high,
Where strenuous youth had scored the runes of hidden power
Not easily read ; a mouth pliant for speech, an eye
Whose ambushed fires at need could terribly outleap
In menace or command, mastering the wills of men.

He wore upon him all the colours of a King
By ancient laws ordained : the three colours, the white,
Crimson, and black ; with these blending, by ancient law,
The four colours, the red, yellow, and green, and blue,
Enriched with gleaming gold.   But subtly Conchobar
Loved to display the seven fair colours of a King,
Inwoven and intertwined in traceries quaint and rare ;
And his keen eye would search the play of shimmering hues,
Even as his ear the turns and tricks of tuneful art
Of skilled harpers.   For craft of hand as craft of mind
Was ever his delight, and subtle as his mind
Ever his dress.   No King in splendour was his peer,
Each looked a gaudy clown, at vie with Conchobar.

Over his chair of state four silver posts upheld
A silken canopy ; and by him were his arms :
'The Hawk,' his casting-spear, that never left his hand
But death sang in its scream ; and, in its jewelled sheath,
His sword, 'Flame of the Sea,' won by his sires, of yore,
From some slain Eastern King—the blade, with wizard spells,
Tempered in magic baths under the Syrian moon.
But in the House of Arms, bode his long thrusting-spear,
'Spoil-winner' ; there too bode, far famed in bardic song,
'The Bellower,' his great shield, seven-bossed, whose pealing voice,
Loud o'er the battle's roar, would call its vassal waves,
The wave of Toth, the wave of Rury, and the wave
Of Cleena, the three waves, to thunder on their shores,
Ireland's three magic waves, at danger of her King.

On the High-King's right hand sat Cathvah, that white peer
Of hoary Time, like Time wrinkled and hoar ; the beard
Upon his breast, the hair upon his druid head
Wintered with eld ; Cathvah, whose voice was like the sea's
For mystery and awe, and like the brooding sea
Blue were his druid eyes, and sad with things to come.

And on his left was set old Shancha of the Laws,
His Councillor ; none lived wiser in all the lore
Of state-craft, and the laws and customs of old time.
Thin was his shaven face ; deep under the black brows
Gleamed his keen eyes that weighed coldly each thing they saw ;
Long was his head and high, fringed round with silver hair ;
Smooth as an egg above, where baldness on the dome
Sat in grave state, yet looked no blemish where it sat.
These two after the King were honoured in the hall.

On wings of song flew by the hastening day, and song
Led in the hooded night, soft stealing on the feast;
And without stint the wife of Felimy the Bard
Crowned the great horn with ale, with mead the golden cup,
To circle the great hall. Praised for her open hand,
She served with nimble cheer, though now her hour drew nigh.

But when the hearts of all were merry, and their brains
Hummed with the humming ale, and drowsily the harps
Murmured of deeds long done, till sleep with downy wing
Fanned heavy lids, a cry, a thin keen shuddering cry,
Rang eerily through the hall, dumbing all tongues, for lo!
Foreboding birth's dread hour, loud shrieked the babe unborn.

Then cheeks grew pale that ne'er in danger's grimmest hour
Failed of their wholesome red; and ghastly looks met looks
As ghastly in the eyes of champions whose proud names
Were songs of valour. First came loosing of the tongue
To Felimy. His words shook on the breath of fear:
'Woman, what woeful voice that rends my heart like steel
Keenes from thee now?' His wife with trembling hands of prayer
Sank pale at Cathvah's feet: 'From what night-shrieking wraith,
O Druid, came that voice? A hand of ice is laid
Upon my heart: the keene comes to the house of death!'

And Cathvah said: 'A child cries in the gate of birth
For terror of this world; yet shall she be the queen
Of all this world for beauty. Ushered by fear she comes,
And "Dread" shall be her name; Deirdrè I name her now,
For dear shall Eri dree her beauty and her birth.'

Then, with her pangs upon her, the mother from the hall
Was hurried by her maids; and ere they rose that night
A wail was in the house, for Death came to that birth,
And Deirdrè's mother passed with the coming of her child.

Anon the aged crones that haunt with equal feet
The house of joy or tears, priestesses hoar like-skilled
In rites of death or birth, solemnly up the hall
Paced slow, bearing the babe; and with a weeping word,
'Thy dead wife sends thee this,' laid it in its father's arms.
And Felimy bent down, and dazed with sudden grief,
Kissed it without a tear.   Then Cathvah took the child
And o'er its new-born head murmured his druid song:

THE DRUID SONG OF CATHVAH.

1.

O Deirdrè, terrible child,
For thee, red star of our ruin,
Great weeping shall be in Eri,
Woe, woe, and a breach in Ulla!

2.

The flame of thy dawn shall kindle
The pride of Kings to possess thee,
The spite of Queens for thy slander:
In seas of blood is thy setting.

3.

War, war is thy bridesmaid,
Thou soft, small whelp of terror;
Thy feet shall trample the mighty,
Yet stumble on heads thou lovest.

4.

The little heap of thy grave
Shall dwell in thy desolation ;
Sad songs shall wail over Eri
Thy dolorous name, O Deirdrè !

To the nurse he gave the child.   In silence from the hall
Deirdrè was borne.   Anon the vast hush of the night
Was filled with dreadful sound : the shield of Conchobar,
Raising its brazen voice within the House of Arms,
Bellowed ; and at its call a mighty voice they knew
Thundered from the far shore, the voice of the great wave
Of Rury.   And the voice of the great wave of Toth,
And the great wave of Cleena, answered him from afar,
Thundering upon their shores at danger of their King.

They heard, and faces stern grimly about the board
Met in pale questioning fear faces as stern ; and all
The house murmured, and sounds of wrathful note were heard,
Boding a storm.   Then rose an old grey wolf of war,
And said : 'An evil babe is born this night in Ulla,
Crush dragons in the egg, be Deirdrè but a dream.'

And so from tongue to tongue that name of fear was tost,
'Deirdrè !'   And many cried : 'Slay her !'   Fierce with vague
    dread,
Bayed in full cry the Hounds of Ulla for the blood
Of one weak babe.   Then well for Deirdrè that her nurse
Fled with her from the house : a hundred swords had else,
Gashing in savage haste her beauty's tender bud,
Stilled her small cry : so fierce is panic in the brave !

But Felimy, who sat dumb in the sudden storm,
Sprang to his feet, and pale, with trembling hand essayed
His branch's tremulous rain of golden sound.   Meanwhile
Conchobar mused ; but now his inward-beaming eye
Lightened athwart the din, as with firm hand he smote
The silver sounding-dish hung by his chair, and woke
The sweet commanding voice of music in the plate,
And thrice he struck, and made the silence of a King.

And frowning down the board, and with stern voice, as when
From a mean quarry in scorn the huntsman calls his pack :
' What scares you thus?' he cried.   ' Shall we, warriors, whose life
Is war, for fear of wars run mad?   Shame on the sword
That leaps not in defence of valour's golden prize ! '

Then to his host he turned, and said : ' O Felimy,
This child will be the flower of all the world, a thing
Unsistered, terrible.   Before the face of Kings
Danger should quail : I claim thy daughter's perilous hand,
Black be his grave who wrongs the bride of Conchobar ! '

He spoke, and through the night, from the great House of Arms
Sounded with brazen voice, once more, his mighty shield,
' The Bellower,' with dread roar calling its vassal waves,
The wave of Toth, the wave of Cleena, and the wave
Of Rury—the three waves, to thunder on their shores,
Ireland's three magic waves, at danger of her King.

Then, in the wondering hush of guests, the Bard looked up.
' Take her,' sighed Felimy ; ' on me and on my house
Her danger fall : on thee and Ulla shine her grace ! '
And mournfully in its house murmured the groaning shield,
Mournfully on their shores moaned the three druid waves.

'What sayest thou to my waves, Cathvah?' said Conchobar.
And Cathvah smiled on him a sad and flickering smile:
'Hold her, O King, thou hast dominion in thy hand,
Lose her, and with her goes thy glory and thy power.'

'Now, by the *Ard-roth*, my brooch where sits my sovereignty,
A good word,' said the King, 'O Cathvah, is that word!
What nobler bride could King desire, that wears upon him
A battle-winning sword?   Great is the doom and stern
That on thy tongue this night chimes with my heart's high song:
Loud let the waves thunder my Deirdrè's dreadful name!'

He spoke, and with bold voice challenged the woe to come,
Down the great hall his eyes lightening in sudden scorn;
And harp and voice acclaimed the choice of the High-King.
So Deirdrè came, so passed the perilous gates of birth.

THE SECOND DUAN.

THE FOSTERING OF DEIRDRÈ.

So Deirdrè kept her life, and in her childhood's years
Throve like a slender plant of willow by a stream.
And for his chosen bride's close keeping, Conchobar
Built on a heathery isle, set in a lonely mere
Deep in the woods, a house: a Queen's fair sunny house
Of odorous pine; the walls with osier wattled round,
The roof over them thatched with silvery reeds, the doors
Plated and hinged with bronze, the door-posts and the beams
Carven, and painted bright with woad and cinnabar.

The rooms were lined within with scales of bronze, low seats
Ran benchwise round the walls.   The bed shone like a Queen's,
With broidered coverlets; and silver posts upheld
A silken canopy, over the pillows' down
Where the small golden head might sink in hollows warm
Of happy sleep.   The floors were strown with rushes green
From bending river-banks, and skins of mighty beasts
Slain in the dew of the morn in many a noble chase.

A southward-looking porch the house had, for the joy
Of the sweet air, the roof thatched all with sea-birds' wings
Dyed yellow and ruddy brown, and ranged to please the eye
In patterns quaint, as fits the dwelling of a Queen.
And when the summer winds played in that porch, no wind
But brought upon his wings the smell of summer days,
Smell of sweet clover, thyme, hot furze, or heather-bells.

Before the porch they made a lawn of pleasant grass
On a sunned slope, wherein seven rowans waved their boughs,
To keep the house from harm; beyond it, by the mere,
Planting an orchard-plot with goodly apple-trees.

East of the house they made within a sheltered nook
A garden of sweet herbs and druid plants; thereby
A bee-yard, rich in hives, where many a buzzing swarm,
That made the island loud all day with summer sound,
Stored the sweet honey; and near, a mead-house with its vats.

West of the house they built a well-thatched byre of cows,
And milking-shed, and set house-leek upon the roof,
To bring good luck and fend the sheds from plague and fire,
And all about the walls sovarchy, with green leaves
And golden stars, to keep from elfin-blasts the cows.

And tall above the house upon the north-side stood
A noble ash, the tree of queens ; and on the north,
A dairy, fresh and cool, with many pans for milk
And white well-scalded churns ; and vervain by the door
They set, lest fairy-spells might fall upon the churns ;
For vainly toil the maids when butter is bewitched.

And all about the mere that circled Deirdrè's isle
Wide was the woodland space fenced in on every side.
And there dwelt at their will all innocent wild things ;
There roamed the great red-deer ; there in close covert played
Blithe hares ; there in the stream, its rooty banks the home
Of burrowing water-rats, the sleek shy otter plunged ;
There frisked the squirrel ; there the blackbird and the thrush
With music filled the woods.   For there might no man come
With noise of baying hound, or wind the blustering horn ;
No sling might hurl, no spear thrust, or swift falcon fly.

So, first of Irish Kings, did royal Conchobar
This royal park ordain ; and on his chiefs he laid
A Champion's Vow : that none, roaming the wood, might come
Within three sling-shots near the fortress of his Love.

There Deirdrè's rathe beauty, like some bright fatal flower,
Earth and the gendering sun conspire with hoary Time
To bring at destined hour to birth, ripened unseen,
Her father dead ; unseen, save of her foster-sire
And Cathvah and the King.   Alone of men these three
In the wood's heart beheld the Child of Doom.   These three
Alone of men, long years, the child saw ; and with these
Two women only, her whose breast had fostered her,
And crafty Lavarcam, the Conversation-Dame,
The ear of Conchobar, who gleaned him day by day
The tattle of all tongues, whence all men's minds he knew.
So grew the child unseen, the realm's forgotten dread.

These few, and the wild tribes of her familiar woods,
Were Deirdrè's world; and free, sequestered in those woods
Since first her step grew firm, she roamed; fearless and free
As the wild things she loved.   There happily her young life,
Fresh as the ranging air she breathed, under all skies,
Throve in the seasons four, knowing the season's change.
No sorcery of the moon she feared, no blazing stroke
Of sun, cold kiss of rain, or tingling pinch of frost.
The whispering Spring she knew, great Summer's golden joy,
Autumn's rich hoarded sweets, stern Winter's cupboards bare,
And gentler than the hunter's was her woodcraft's lore.

Cathvah she loved, and him, in her dead father's place,
She honoured most; but when the King, in whose grave soul
Her beauty's bright increase wrought like a Druid's charm,
Dreaming her his, would come in his rare hours of ease
To gaze on her and feel the billows of his blood,
Warmed in her splendour, heave with mightier youth, would she
Frown like a captive Queen, donning her haughtiest look,
And, dauntless, with cold eyes outstare the gazing King.

Then, like a bird set free, when Conchobar at last
Left her, the mutinous blood hot in her angry cheek,
She would run to Lavarcam, crying in childish rage:
' Bad is this King of yours, Fergus shall be my King!
There is an evil-eye in Conchobar, I hate him!
Poison is on his tongue, bale in his eyes' blue flame;
His passing makes the flowers droop in the woods; the birds
Fear him, and in the leaves cower when he comes, as when
The kestrel's shadow falls upon them.   Comes he here
Me with his sorcerer's eyes to blight?   Let him beware!
I am a Druid's child—let him beware of me!'

And Lavarcam would soothe her moods with honeyed words.
She loved the passionate child, still flattering Conchobar
With hopes answering his dreams.   But Deirdrè read her guile,
And early learnt to charm the secrets from her tongue.

From her she had heard the tale of Fergus : how he reigned
O'er Ulster in his right ; but, being of jovial mind,
Hunting, of all things else, after the glorious game
Of war, and those great songs that won him high renown
As King among the Bards, and Bard among the Kings,
He dearly loved ; and next the splendour of great feasts,
Where mighty ale abounds, and keen three-cornered harps,
Harps with a woman's soul of sadness or wild mirth,
Cry sweetly in the hands of skilled harpers, and Bards
Chant the great deeds of old, or the long line of Kings :
And for his vow he had : *Ne'er to refuse a feast.*

And how his heart was set madly in love on one,
Fachtna's young widowed Queen, Nessa the Fair, forlorn
In Tara, where her lord, Fachtna the Wise, High-King
Over all Erin, fell by the prevailing sword
Of Eocha of the Sighs ; and how he took her thence
With blue-eyed Conchobar, her only child, and brought her
For love to his own court.   And there, on days of law
When the King sat and heard causes, beside his chair
The boy with keen blue eyes would mark the litigants,
And sit listening, and hear the pleadings, and the King's
Judgment on all.   And once when Fergus heard a suit
With tangled points of law, *ollav* 'gainst *ollav* matched
Wrangling with tongues more sharp than women's at a fair,
The King in sudden chafe burst out : ' Where hides this day
The hare of truth in all this prickly field of furze ?
She sits too close for me.   But when the old hound's at fault,
The whelp may find : come, boy, track her for us, my son ! '

Then Conchobar stood forth, and gravely, without haste,
Untwined the tangled skein, all doubtful points of law
Set clear, and, handling all, said modestly at last :
‘ With favour of the King, and this High Court, had I
The voice of judgment here, thus my award should fall.’

Then rang the court with shouts : ‘ Long life to Conchobar,
True is your tongue, my son ! ’   And Fergus, who had stared
Amazed upon the boy, clapped on his shoulder now
His sunburnt sword-hand, laughed his laugh that all men loved,
And cried : ‘ Now, by my hand of valour ! here’s a boy
That ousts me from my seat, the judge’s judge, the King
Of the High-King !   My arm can wield the spears of war ;
But here’s a head of gold, born with an *ollav’s* gown
For caul upon its brows, a brain to drive my brain
As I my war-horse.’   So spake Fergus truth in jest.

For ever from that day with all her woman’s might,
And all her woman’s craft, strove Nessa to make true
These words of Fergus.   First, Conchobar at the court
Was ever at his side prompting his ruling ; then
He sat his deputy ; at last in his high place
Alone he sat, High-King.   Fergus, for Nessa’s love,
Gave him, from his own breast, the brooch of royalty
The great *Ard-Roth ;* and took the belt of royal power
From his own loins ; and gave the *cathbarr* from his head,
To flame on his young brow in golden majesty.
So laughed away his realm the man of glorious heart.

Then Lavarcam crooned on to Deirdrè of the wives
Of Conchobar : how first spear-bearing Meave he took,
With a rich dower of all that Kings delight in : arms,
Chariots, horses and hounds, cloaks, brooches, cups of gold,

And gold that buys the world.   From her great father's hand,
Dark Eocha of the Sighs, spear-bearing Meave he took,
With all her dowry, given in eric for the death
Of his own father, slain by Eocha.   But red Meave,
Haughty of soul, desired to plant her warrior feet
Upon the necks of Kings, and Conchobar she deemed
An *Ollav* of the courts: men he could rule, but her,
His wife, he could not rule.   Great was the spleen that stirred
Between them, till she fled, in hate of Conchobar,
Back to her father's house; and Eocha gave her then
Lands by the Shannon, south of Easroe, to the sea,
To hold in her own right, even all the Firbolg's land
In Olnemachta.   There she reigned in her own right,
Red Meave, the warrior Queen, in scorn of Conchobar.

But her war-wearied sire in Meave's forsaken bed,
With a new dowry claimed by Conchobar, put now
Enna, her sister—mild her mind, and short her life;
Two sons she bore the King, then, with a widowed heart
She left him in his prime.   So Deirdrè day by day
Heard at her will, well pleased, the tales of Lavarcam.

Cathvah too loved the child, and of his hoary craft
Taught her the lore of the woods, and the lore of sun and moon,
And the lore of the druid stars, seasons and lucky days,
Omens, and charms, and spells, and secret cures.   And oft
He would take his harp, and sing of old-world names and deeds:
Of Ireland's seven great names, a flower of glory each one,
For each, deep in her breast, a sorrow and a sword.

So Deirdrè heard the song of Cathvah, the grey seer;
And at his bardic song of Ireland's olden fame,
Great names, and sounding deeds of yore, her virgin heart,
Exulting in high thoughts, leaped high, daring her doom.

THE THIRD DUAN.

THE SONS OF USNA.

Tall grew the child, and learnt of Cathvah, day by day,
New things : all sleights of song she learnt, and of the harp
Mastery in all the modes ; and gracefully to wield
The weapons of a Queen ; to run, to leap, to dance ;
And in the woods she poured, in gusts of sudden song,
The passion of her heart, like the glad birds, and made
Old tales and heroes dead in her lone childish sports
To live again, peopling the world with her young dreams.

These things she loved ; nor less the lore of Lavarcam,
Whose tongue, in quiet hours beside the 'broidery frame,
Flew faster than her hand.   But oft some tale of love,
And lover's piteous fates, murmuring in Deirdrè's ear
Made trouble in her heart ; and as the virgin bud
Of her wild beauty swelled in ripening womanhood,
Roaming the woods alone, the pageant of her dreams
Grew eager with new shapes, bright faces ; and the trees
Sighed with some fond desire, some wordless want.   Each dawn
And glowing even breathed rich glamour that made pale
Old druidries.   And now long hours in the sweet woods
Dumb would she lie, and dream ; amorous of the brooding sky,
And of the glorious sun, amorous of eve's lone star,
Amorous of the sighing winds, amorous of the whispering trees,
And the streams murmuring still that word of mystery : Love.

At last there came a day, her seventeenth summer flown,
When Conchobar beheld her glowing in his eye,
A woman grown, the bride of his long dream. He smiled,
Commanding Lavarcam to ply her woman's craft,
And charm with honeyed words the maiden's fancy now
To soar to royal heights, and circle round her King.

So next when Deirdrè came, a sadness in her eyes
That strove to fathom fate, questioning of Lavarcam:
'Why do they keep me here, a captive, out of sight
Of the great world of deeds, where men contend with men,
And bards beholding find new splendid themes for song?'
No more did Lavarcam essay to put her by
With words to please a child, but cunningly answered her.
'Show me your hand,' she said, 'I'll read your destiny.
The world will kiss that hand; for here, pulse of my heart,
High fortune waits for you, bound in your line of fate.
Ah Deirdrè, would you be the bride of a great King?'

'A King?' she said, and pride flamed in her answering eye,
To meet the call of her fate; the swelling of her soul
Heaved proudly her young breast, one moment. Then the blood
Fled from her cheek; she frowned and bent on Lavarcam
A flashing look, and stern, tenting her to the thought.
'A King!' she cried again, 'Conchobar is a King:
Is it he? Is it for himself that he has mewed me here,
Like a tame falcon? Ay, I see it in your eyes.'

Then Lavarcam essayed with all her guile to lure
This wild hawk from her flight. Like honey from her lips
Words fair in promise fell in Deirdrè's angry ear.
'Where'er she comes my pearl shall set her beauty's feet
On fairest necks,' she vowed, 'the necks of envious Queens

Out-rivalled!   O'er the land sage harps shall sound your praise
At lordly ale-feasts where the voice of song is loud ;
And you shall have withal the love of this great King ! '

She spoke of the long love of royal Conchobar,
A steadfast-burning star, of radiance to outshine
The flame of meaner hearts : a great King in his prime,
The phantom fires of youth burnt out, the genial heat
Of his wise manhood all aglow for one rare maid,
Born for his bride ! ' Could maid sigh for a happier fate ? '

' For this ye have reared me, then ! ' cried Deirdrè, white with scorn,
And fled in wrath to the woods.   There in a ferny dell
She raged at Fate : ' I—I, the bride of Conchobar !
Liars were the hopes of the day, liars the dreams of the night,
That never told me this !   Sere are the leaves that hang
On that grey tree of love, now budding new for me,
The heart of Conchobar.   Meave was a withered leaf
Blown by in passion's gust before my birth, and cold
Poor Enna mouldering lies.   They are old songs, these loves
Of royal Conchobar, and now he sisters me
With wrinkled Meave, long since fled in the days of yore
Back to her father's house, for hatred of her lord.
I have no father.   Oh ! liars are the golden tales
So dear to memory, tales that tell how youth mates youth :
Some maid like me, some King like Conchobar—some youth,
Love's morning in his face, comes boldly ranging by ;
Then troubles she no more the King's house with her sighs.
Who comes for me ?   Where roams my love ? '   An eagle then
Swooped on a shuddering hare, stilling her shriek with death ;
And Deirdrè saw, sighing, as, with the drooping thing
Gript in his talons, up the bird soared, and was gone.

' There soars the great High-King,' she mused, ' and in his gripe
Holds my slain heart—no help for the weak things of the world !
I will be strong and bold, or, even though weak still bold ;
No man in arms unloved shall wind me—better death ! '

Thereat a questing wind came rustling through the leaves
Sering to Autumn, whirled a score away, and passed,
Seeming to whisper : ' Death,' in answer to her thought ;
The word of mystery, Death, breathed where so lately breathed
The word of mystery, Love.   And Deirdrè, sad and slow,
Paced through the murmuring wood back to her house of pine.

That Autumn Conchobar was absent in new wars
With vassal Kings, and left, his regent o'er the realm,
Fergus ; but e'er he marched from Eman's Green ordained
His marriage for the Spring, and Deirdrè, grave and pale,
Received his trothal-gifts, and visit of farewell,
Bowing her to his will, it seemed, without a word.

But all that Autumn through sadly she looked, like one
Wandering in ways of gloom, and, dark to Lavarcam,
Brooded, and little spoke, save when at times she grew
Restless and sharp of tongue, and suddenly in her face
Would flash strange questions ; then, ere the good dame surprised
Could find a smooth reply, would leave her where she stood,
And rush in sullen rage to scour the woods all day,
Hunting.   She loved to prove her weapon's might on all
The noble beasts of chase ; thinking within her heart
' All things are strong or weak, cruel is life to the weak,
I will be strong,' she ranged the woods on tireless feet,
While with her to the chase went Conchobar's great hound,
Congal, and with her went her foster-father, keen
To guard her from ill-hap, and proud to find his child
So apt in arms.   And thus the Autumn passed away.

E

Meanwhile to Fergus came this word from the High-King:
That, even in Winter's teeth still obstinate in war,
Bide would he where he lay, in a strong place far off,
Waiting the Spring, to force the Kings from their last hold.

Then Winter fell, and long the land lay whelmed in snow;
And in the snow the wolves came prowling round the lake;
And Deirdrè, in fair fight, deft spear 'gainst furious fangs,
Slew more than one, laughing to see her grim grey foe
Rage his fierce life away in blood shed by her hand.

One day she chanced to pass with Lavarcam where lay
A beast new slain.   And there a raven in the snow
Gorged the fresh blood.   Thereat the fire in Deirdrè's breast
Long smouldering flamed in words, for its deep longing's sake
Defying all the world.   Reckless of Lavarcam,
The sigh of her soul burst forth: ' Black be my lover's hair
As yon bold raven's wing, the red and white in his cheek
Blend as yon blood and snow—none else shall have my love!'

New light shone in her eyes, her beauty glowed, new-born,
In her young passionate face.   The heart of Lavarcam
Smiled in her; for it held old spite 'gainst Conchobar,
For slights the moody King, she deemed, had cast on her,
And Deirdrè she adored.   ' Fair fall your maiden choice!'
She said, humouring her charge.   ' That very man I know,
Naisi, old Usna's son—hair like the raven's wing,
And the pure colours blend more softly in his cheek
Than blood with snow.   There walk, indeed, no better men
On the world's ridge, this day, than Usna's three stout Sons.
O, you should see the three, for sport, on Eman's Green,
Back to back, sword in hand, their shields before them thrown,
Hold all the Province, ranged against them, a full hour
In check with warlike play!   Their leaping like the roe's

For lightness; and for weight their rushing like the bull's;
Their sword-play like the thrust of lightning when it strikes,
Unseen for swiftness! Hounds tireless they are in chase,
None swifter: in the plain they can run down the buck,
And take him by the horns alive. And great they are
In song, great harpers too; their music stills the storm,
Draws a man's heart from his breast, and charms the very cows
To brim the pails with milk, such flattery's in the sound.

'Well, you are Conchobar's; but were I young this day
I could choose. Usna's sons can carry it with the best,
All three: Naisi the Bold, Ainli the Swift of Foot,
Ardàn of the Sweet Voice. For beauty—why they daunt
The eye that looks on them, like the sun's face in heaven!
But Naisi's King of them all, King of the three, for shape,
Beauty of face, and all that makes a man a man.
Why do I tell you this? Ah! sure such men as these
Make a poor woman's tongue break loose out of her head,
Even mine that should be curbed twice over here with you;
For you are Conchobar's, that's sure. But in his court
You must see men, the Sons of Usna with the rest;
But guard your heart, my child, ay, guard your heart, I say.'

Then Deirdrè sighed and said: 'Till I have sight of him
You set so high, Naisi, I shall have ease no more.'
And slyly Lavarcam spoke in her ear: 'Well, well,
Give us but smiles for sighs, you *shall* have sight of him.'

Spring came, and Conchobar, victorious in his wars,
Sent Conall Carnach first, leading the vanguard, home
Laden with spoil; and soon the flower of Eman's youth
Came with Cuchullin back; the King, with half his power,
Tarrying to fix his yoke on the submitted Kings.

So with Cuchullin came the sons of Usna home,
Naisi the Bold, Ainli the Swift of Foot, and last
Ardàn of the Sweet Voice.   Anon came Lavarcam
Whispering in Deirdrè's ear : ' The sun is back in heaven,
The lusty Spring is here, and Naisi's home again.
Now think on Conchobar ; for you shall see *my* Love.'

And soon it chanced one day that Naisi's deer-hound ran
Into the King's close wood : the youth on eager foot
Followed her ere he knew, and coaxed her to the leash.
Then on the forest's bound, glad of the sunshine there,
In a wide furzy space, sweet with the breath of Spring,
Sat down awhile, to feel his heart of gladness leap
At Spring's first kiss.   The lark sang in the sky, the blackbirds
Were warbling in the woods ; and as he sat alone
He sang like any bird, as carelessly and loud.

But Lavarcam, whose craft followed his going, sure
As hound his master's trail, with word of where he lay
Sought Deirdrè, crying : 'Come !   The rarest bird of spring
Sings in the woods to-day ! '   And swiftly to the woods
She led her from the field wherein she walked, a ball
Of cowslips in her hand—swiftly on fatal feet
Hurrying her away, to meet with Naisi, and her doom.

So they drew near the spot where Naisi in the furze
Still sat and sang ; and Deirdrè, ere she saw him, heard
His voice filling the air with jubilant song.   Her heart
Failed in the flood of sound, that seemed to claim the world
With its bold manhood : tears sprang in her eyes, her breast
Swelled, as she strove with some new rapture, wild to o'erleap
The bounds of the world.   Anon, with an imperious hand,
Dismissing Lavarcam, forth, like an eaglet fledged,

That feels the mighty wind's keen summons in her wings,
And sinks upon the unknown abyss of air, she went
Forth from the woods; and straight to Naisi where he sat
Came, like a wild thing lured, looked on him, and passed by.

And Naisi, as she came, ceased from his song, amazed;
For, by him as she went, her beautiful wild face
Faintly aglow, the shy dews of a love new-born
Soft in her glorious eyes, she flashed on him a look
Wistful and strange. The youth sprang from his lair, and made
One step, as though his feet must follow her, murmuring low:
'Fair is the doe that finds a covert in these woods!'

Thereat she suddenly turned, facing him with a smile,
And answered: 'Foul or fair, what recks the doe, where hart
May never range?' And Naisi knew Deirdrè, and stood
Abashed before the bride of Conchobar, whose face
Outshone its whispered fame. The frank unsullied blood
Of a young Irish chief, red in his cheek, proclaimed
His maiden soul, as there, gazing on her, he said,
Low, with a fervent awe: 'A royal stag alone
Mates with a doe so fair, even the great stag whose range
This Province is, and he alone is worth her thought.'

At this, her heart no more fluttering from shy to bold,
But stung to one rash leap, Deirdrè with passionate tongue
Spake all her mind, crying: 'No royal stag for me!
I choose the branchless hart, fit for my love: O thou,
Naisi, on whom these eyes ne'er fell till this great hour,
Thou art my love, my fate, thou—thou—not Conchobar!
Be thou my king, and thine for ever will I be,
Or let me die this day!' Naisi amazed, as though
The sun out of the sky wooed him with passionate words,
Drew back, murmuring: 'Nay, nay, Maiden, this cannot be;

For so should fall the curse that Cathvah's druid tongue
Foretold should come one day by thee upon this Land.'
She frowned.   ' In that ill word thou wouldst refuse my love ? '
' I must ! ' sighed he, and stood before her with bowed head.

' He scorns me ! ' Deirdrè thought, and white with sudden wrath,
Flung in his face the ball of cowslips that she held,
Crying : ' I thought to find Naisi the Bold, and find
A coward !   Be this blow, dealt by a woman's hand,
Disgrace, through thy life's length ! ' ' Ah Deirdrè let me go ! '
He answered, ' or disgrace will fall upon thee first,
And this fair Land through thee.' ' Take then thy sword,' she said,
' And slay me now, and go—if go thou wilt.   Here, here ! '

She stood, her maiden breast heaving beneath her hand,
And proudly claimed the stroke.   And Naisi, in the shame
Her dauntless passion bred, feeling that passion's flood
Surge over him like flame, blushed like a maid half-won,
And spoke not.   Then her hand upon his arm she laid,
Saying : ' Nay, take me hence, I charge thee—on thy vow
Ne'er to refuse thine aid to wretches in distress.'
And he : ' Thou hast thy will.   There was no other word
Could move me ; for the sake of Ulla, that by us
Must suffer many woes.   Yet I know well thy love
Is worth a world.'   They kissed, and Deirdrè spoke again :
' I am a Druid's child, and Cathvah's secret lore
Is mine.   Trust me the weird of Druids is no weird
For souls resolved and stern.   Let kingdoms rise and fall,
But us two love.'   ' Be it so,' said Naisi, ' O farewell
The Red Branch House, farewell to Eman's Green !   To-night
We must be far away, alone, or with my Clan.'

He strode into the sun, and raised his rallying cry:
'To my side, Clan Usna!' And soon came bursting thro' the furze
Ainli, the Swift of Foot, and Ardàn. Naisi then
Took Deirdrè by the hand, and said: 'Brothers, this day
My fate calls me in this fair woman ye see here,
Deirdrè, to whom my heart is bound with such a band
As only death can loose. Make ye your choice, of me
Or Conchobar.' The twain were troubled at his words,
And Ainli said: 'No need to speak of Conchobar:
We are thy men—thy kin, the seed of one great sire,
Of one dear mother born. But now where lies our way?
What thing is this thou dost? Bad were it any man
Our comrade of the Branch, board-sharer with us all,
Should, wounding thee, do well, wounding thee for thy fault!'

'But Deirdrè,' Naisi said, 'has laid on me my vow,
That I shall take her hence. What must be, let it be.'
They sighed, and said: 'Be it so! Evil will come of this,
Yet no disgrace be thine. There is no King so great,
Sits on the ridge of the world who would not see with joy
The shining of our swords come to him. Where we go
Great welcome shall we have. Farewell to Conchobar!'

To Deirdrè then they came and made her kiss their swords,
And kissed them after her. 'Sword-sister shalt thou be
To Usna's sons, and blood our swords shall drink, ere tears
Redden thine eyes. Thy name, O Deirdrè, shall be dread
Unto thy foes.' That night went Usna's three stout Sons,
And Deirdrè as the fourth, from Eman, with a band
Of three times fifty men, and three times fifty hounds,
Women and serving-men. Ere Fergus woke next morn,
The four were far away. So Deirdrè spurned the love
Of Conchobar, and fled with Naisi and his Clan.

THE FOURTH DUAN.

THE RED KING.

'With the three traitor Sons of Usna, and their Clan
Deirdrè is fled from thee.'   This word to Conchobar
Came suddenly as he sat with Shancha, the great judge
In a sage court of Bards, Ollavs, and Shanachies ;
Laying on the conquered Kings his law.   Sternly he read
The secret message, tied by Fergus in the twine
Of knotted rushes, tore, and cast it from his hand,
Without a word ; nor stayed the business of the court
Till all was fairly done ; then gave command to strike
The camp that hour, for a forced march, back to the North.

Fierce was his wrath ; for deep the passion that possessed
His lonely soul, wherein Deirdrè's young beauty dwelt,
A hidden sorceress, singing ever a magic song
That mingled in the hum of busy thoughts.   And now
His house of dreams was like a house of fallen Kings,
Ruined and full of gloom, and through the gloom he heard
Memory reword the saw that Cathvah darkly spake
O'er Deirdrè's new-born head—each word burnt in his brain :
' *Hold her, O King, thou hast dominion in thy hand ;
Lose her, and with her goes thy glory and thy power.*'
And the Banshee, Despair, came wailing round his heart :
' Lost ! lost ! ' even as he rode amidst the armed clang
Of marching men whose feet devoured the way like fire.

By day men went in fear of the King's face ; and never
Twixt him and Fergus passed words of such bitter sting
As now ; till Fergus wept for sorrow and for shame ;
Yet open breach as yet was none between the two.

And Lavarcam, the Dame of honeyed lips, was fain
To grovel at his feet like a whipt hound ; but naught
Availed her honeyed words ; and banished from the Court
A year in solitude she pined, and black disgrace. .

But night alone beheld his lonely rage, and heard
His moan, like some strong wounded beast's, boding his foes
Danger.   Great was his heart, great its wound, great its groan :
' Laughter is in my ears this night, shame on my cheek !
I have done great deeds in vain ; in vain my walk of power
Has been with Druids hoar, and Ollavs sage in law ;
In vain I have made the Bards of Erin rich as Kings,
Gathered them round me, filled with the desire of hearts
Their Pot of Avarice !   Now, in every mouth of gold
Mocked shall I be.   My name of glory shall be made
The quarry of the world, hunted by currish tongues,
Slain by a jesting word, mangled about the court
Of Kings it frighted.   Red, red are the wings of shame
Above me !   Red sit shame, for this, upon your brows,
Usna's three traitor Sons ; red be the bed of your death,
Bloody the day ye meet the hounds of my revenge !
Glad shall the carrion kites be for thy sake, that day,
Naisi ; thy cheeks that feed a woman's wanton lips
Shall have the crows for kissers.   Day shall be scant of light
For your fleeing, night of gloom to hide you from my hate.

' And she, Deirdrè, O she—closer she bound my heart
Than binds my loins with power the belt of royalty !
From Erin's budding skies the sun fled, when she fled ;
Gloomy she leaves the woods, stumbling of feet she plants
In the firm ways of a king ; whereby to earth must come
Many fair heads.   For her I'll flood the silver streams
Of Banba with men's blood, the best of all my realm,

But I must have her back!   Bloody in sooth shall be
Our wooing, Flower of the Woods, Flower of the World—salt tears
Flow at our bridal!   Songs more fierce and stern than songs
Of satirists shall be made about us ; but the King
Will have his own, or lose his kingdom with his bride.'
Thus moaned his mighty heart, as in the sleepless hours
About his lonely bed paced still, with pallid lips
Murmuring in slakeless thirst, the wraith of his revenge.

Deirdrè, meanwhile, with Usna's Sons, roamed thro' the land,
A waif, tost on the sea of Conchobar's great wrath ;
For none durst shelter long the exiles, hunted still
From Easroe in the West even to that eastern bay
Where looks Ben Edar o'er the strait of Manannàn.

Yet happy was her life, keen with the bliss of her love
For Naisi—strong the love she kindled in his heart,
Making the youth a man, the man a king of men :
And Naisi's brothers were like brothers of her blood.
And merrily lived the four, mocking the gusts of fate ;
Sweet rang their harps, and sweet their songs roved thro' the land.

But ease never they had, because of Conchobar,
Till, finding on the coast five galleys, swift of sail,
They shipped for Alba, weighed in a fair wind, and sped
Northward, 'twixt shore and shore ; gay was their cheer, as fast
Their galleys o'er the sea raced by the druid Isle
Of Manannàn ; and soon, over the foaming prow,
Blue rose the mountain crests of Alba of the Lakes,
And safe they came to port, and safely won the shore.

There, in the upland wilds, a space of forest land
They found, where on a hill they built a mighty dun,
Ditched round for their defence ; and merrily bayed their hounds
And far afield they ran in that brisk mountain air,
And none to say them nay, in forest or on fell.

There, in her Alban home, a mother, ere the dream
Of motherhood well had woke to startle in her breast
The girlhood lingering there, young Deirdrè gazed with awe
Into her first-born's face—a lusty boy, she named
Gaier, 'the Hound,' strong whelp of the strong Race of Hounds
His father came of. Thus the Clan lived by the chase,
And when their board was scant of venison, from their hill
They fell upon the plains, and took a spoil of cows.

Then came the men of the plain together, many spears,
To drive the spoilers out ; but Naisi and his Clan,
Leaping among them, fierce as wolves among the flocks,
Did on them terrible deeds. Many they slew, and drove
The remnant in dismay for succour to their King.

To him they came, and said : ' Strangers are in the land,
Who rage like hungry wolves among us, and will soon
Devour us all. On high they have set their mighty dun,
Whence, when desire of meat grows sharp in them, they swoop
Upon our flocks and herds ; and we ourselves are naught
But sheep before the wolf, against them ; for in deeds
They are terrible ; their might is greater than the might
Of the men of Alba. Fierce they are, and run to war
As neighing colts to grass, the shrieking of their spears
Kills us before they strike, the wind of their swift swords
Before they fall. O King, give us thy help to drive
These spoilers from our land, or dead men are we all ! '

Much marvelled then the King to hear this dolorous tale,
Thinking : 'What men are these?   If on the crest of war
Their valour sit so high, great luck it were to gain
For my behoof the might and glamour of their swords.'
Wherefore he sent to them a Druid and a Bard,
To ask their names and race, and give them peace or war.

To Naisi straightway came the heralds of the King,
The Druid and the Bard.   And Usna's Sons in peace
Met them upon the sward before their dun ; and first,
Grave salutation past on both sides, spake the Bard,
Asking : 'What men are ye, and wherefore are ye come,
Like roving wolves of the sea, to spoil our peaceful vales ?'

Quoth Naisi : 'Usna's Sons are we, of the warlike race
Of Rury Mōr.   Full well, at feasts, the Red Branch House
Knows us ; though, twelve months told, blank of our painted
        shields
We have left its walls, flying the wrath of Conchobar,
Our King, who seeks our lives.   No prowlers of the sea
We are ; but warriors, girt like men with trusty swords,
To keep our heads, win land, or take a spoil at need,
When Famine's ugly face comes scowling round our doors ;
And, bring ye peace or war, we shall abide it still
With the fixed mind of men who fear no frown of Fate.'

These words, wherein they saw Naisi had spoken well,
Pleased them ; wonderful too the beauty of the three
Seemed in their eyes.   They drank the rushing mountain air
With the deep lungs of stags, lithe were their brawny arms,
And o'er the sward they stepped with the free port of Kings.

The Druid made reply : ' Whether in peace or war
We come to you, is yours to choose.   Over these vales
May no man range at will, save one, from whom we come,
Our King ; whose power in wrath could sweep your valiant clan
Into the hungry sea.   But why should reckless war
Between us raise this day his bloody crest ?   Our King
Loves a good sword at need, no less than Conchobar,
And rich he is, more land has he than Conchobar,
Lands of the chase, cornland and pasture-land, to fee
Good swords that earn his grace.   If therefore noble war
Ye love, come ye to him ; your spears, whose deadly thirst
Ye have basely slaked in blood of these poor hinds, shall drink
Delight of battle.   Lands lack ye ?   Your swords ere long.
Shall win you land enough, serving our warrior King.'

Good seemed the Druid's words to Naisi ; for the Clan
Were tired of outlawry.   ' Brothers,' he said, ' how looks
This offer, freely made unto us, in your eyes ?
Shall we go serve this King, and wet our spears once more
In dew of glorious war ? '   Said Ainli : ' If this King
Be of good faith herein, he is a King, I trow,
Worth talking with.'   So all agreed upon a day
When—the King pledging first in hostage his two sons—
On a broad river's banks, at either side a ford,
The Chiefs might meet in peace, and come to fuller speech
Touching this compact.   Then, their embassy achieved,
Back to their King returned the Druid and the Bard.

Soon came the trysting-day, when Ainli at the ford
Received the King's two sons, young boys, and to the dun,
Seated like sons of kings with honour in his car,
Bore them, while with their guard crossed Naisi and Ardàn.

In a swift war-car, drawn by battle-snuffing steeds—
Two coal-black stallions foaled amid the wealthiest plains
Of Laigen of the Steeds, fiercer than fire that roars
Under the dun west-wind, in Autumn, through the furze—
The brothers crossed the stream.   Ardàn, with hands of skill
Grasping the reins ashine with silver studs, controlled
The coursers as they rushed in thunder through the ford ;
While with his planted spear stood Naisi, like the mast
Of a King's ship, that sways with its own springy strength
To every gust of the gale, feels all, yet never yields.

So through the ford they rushed, up the steep bank, and stood
A breathing while.   Then slow, the fiery steeds in chafe
Champing their silver bits, till from their lips the foam,
Flecking their shaggy breasts, gleamed like the foam that gleams
On the dark waves of Moyle when the black north-wind blows,
O'er the firm thymy turf they moved to meet the King.

Glorious they moved, as when, gladdening the grass with light,
Walks on a day of cloud a sun-burst o'er the plains ;
And tall they towered as clouds, still giants of the East,
Their heads with sunset crowned ; tall o'er their car, agleam
With bronze and silver : bronze the champion-crushing wheels
And sides of the great car, with silver bossed.   The guard
Marched on each hand ; their shirts were yellow as the flower
Of the sovarchy ; green as the green mane of a brook
In Spring, their woollen cloaks.   Long were the swords they bore,
Stout their shield-piercing spears.   A lance-flight from the King
Ardàn drew up ; lightly the brothers from their car
Leaped, and a-foot went on, a space before their guard.

They came before the King.   A burly man was he,
Red was his face and broad, wide-mouthed and little-eyed,
Blemish of baldness none upon him.   Round his helm
Red stood his bushy hair, red was the beard that curled

Close round his chin.   In strength tough as a bull was he.
He stared upon the chiefs of the Red Branch, and marked
Their well-strung height, their grace, the splendour of their dress,
Their gait, their easy poise and carriage of their arms.

Striding abreast they came; and thus, that day of the days
Long with the days long dead, they looked, their youth's full flower
Upon them.   Champions trained, beautiful, fleet and strong
As deer-hounds in the house of a great King, they looked.
Brown were their faces, brown their sinewy arms, the blood
Rich under their clear skins; brown were their eyes and clear,
And full of lurking light as the deep crystal pool
In Glendalough, that shines below the gleaming fall
Of Poul-an-ass: none clearer shines on the ridge of the world;
But Naisi's held most light.   Black as the blackbird's wing
His hair, in two thick braids, hung to his breast; on each
An apple of bright gold danced blithely to the tune
Of his marching feet; and black upon his cheek and chin
His beard of manhood showed.   Upon his head he wore
A *cathbarr* of white bronze inlaid with beaten gold;
The crest of gold bore high two falcons' wings outspread.

His dark-blue shirt, of wool broidered with threads of gold,
Hung to his knee, below the leathern tunic, bright
With scales of bronze.   In folds from his broad shoulders fell
His mantle of soft wool, crimson in hue : well-boiled
With alder-twigs, to make the madder's gorgeous blood
Bite in the dipping-vats the staple well, that day
Ailve his Mother, bent on household mysteries, fast
Shut herself with her maids into her Sunny House,
Lest eye of man should fall unlucky on the vats
And spoil her dyeing.   Bronze the brooch was at his breast,
Wrought by the elfin hand of Culann, the great smith.

The sword upon his thigh had a great name in war,
Famous as any King's; steel was the blade, long since
Tempered in magic baths under the eastern moon,
Set in a hilt of jade shaped to the grip.   That sword
Given to old Usna once by mighty Manannàn,
Grey wizard of the sea, held in its magic blade
Demons of speech whereby the sword could tell its name,
' Helmbiter'; and the blade held in its edges twain
Demons of sharpness, keen even to divide a hair
On the flowing of a stream.   Three were the swords renowned
In Ireland that same day : Cuchullin's sword, the sword
Of Fergus, and the sword of royal Conchobar ;
And of those three that sword hanging at Naisi's thigh
Was worthy battle-mate, and o'er the din of war
The demons of that sword had often raised their cry,
Answering the battle-cries of the demons of the three.

A stout rib-sheltering shield, defier of the dart,
Bore Naisi, rimmed and bound with bronze inlaid with gold ;
And in his hand he held a mighty spear.   Of bronze
Was the broad-pointed head, casting upon the earth
A shadow like the gloom of death, and long and broad
As a man's grave.   And so came Naisi to the King.

Garbed like a charioteer Ardàn strode at his side ;
A golden fillet, bound about his brow, held back
His long hair from his eyes, a spiral of soft gold
Confined it at the poll.   A linen shirt he wore,
Warm from his mother's loom, and by her loving hand
Broidered at neck and hem and the short sleeves.   His arms,
Sinewy and brown, were bare.   Short from his shoulder hung
His cape of wool, and glowed fresh from his mother's vats

With crimson rich and deep as in October woods
Dyes on their sunny cheeks the clustered crab-apples.
A double stud of gold in eyelets at the breast
Held it. His kilt, below his deer-skin apron's point
Fell to his supple knees in parti-coloured folds.

His whip and goad of bronze his grooms kept in the car,
Thrown by for nobler arms : lightly in his right hand
He bore three hunting-spears, with blades of gleaming bronze
And ashen shafts, the grip well bound with hempen cord.

Behind the brothers came twelve serving-men, and each
Held in the leash a hound, tall as a calf, and swift
As any stag, a torc of gold on every hound
Worth two young cows new-calved, each with her calf; each hound
Worth many a cow. This gift brought Naisi to the King.

Great was the joy the King had in those Irish hounds
Of Naisi's gift. And there, on the broad river-plain
Pleasant with grass, in peace he met the Red-Branch chiefs.
There, after greeting done between them, Naisi's men
Dug with their spears the turf, and raised upon the sward
A sodded seat, whereon sat like an Irish chief
Naisi in state, to close his compact with the King.

Great was the ale-feast made for Naisi by the King,
Great was the joy he had of those two brothers there,
And great his praise of them. For curious were the games
Of war they showed him, each more wondrous than the last.

F

Feats of the spear they showed.   The swallow could not shun
The spear from Ardàn's hand, so swift his casting.   Now
He played with one, now two, now three : the third would leave
His hand while still the first sang in the air, and none
But hit its mark.   The spear that left his hand, his hand
Would catch before it fell, so swift his running.   Bars
A champion's height he cleared, and bars low as his knee
He dived beneath, at speed ; still ever to the King
Saying : 'All this and more does Ainli, Swift of Foot.'

Feats of the sword they shewed ; and Naisi gaged his blade
Against the twelve best blades of Alba.   Then did blade
Ring shrewdly upon blade.   The demons of the swords
Raged in the screaming air, and Naisi's blade became
A dragon in his hand.   The sword it saw, it bit ;
The blade it bit, it broke ; till never a sword durst show
Its teeth against it.   Work did Naisi make that morn
For the Alban smiths ; yet ne'er a sword's tooth of them all
Had gapt his blade.   And next he challenged helms and shields
To meet its flashing swoop ; and never a helm nor shield
Abode a second stroke but three, a third but one,
Saving the King's.   From his the sword leaped screaming back,
And would not bite, such guile of courtesy it could use.

Then turned, for finer play, Naisi its tireless teeth
Of sharpness on the woof of soft and yielding things.
A man's sleeve from his shirt with one swift whirling stroke
He shore, nor razed the skin : a feather in the air,
Met by the hissing steel, floated in twain.   Amazed
The men of Alba stood.   Ne'er had they seen till now
Such sorceries in a sword.   And still, in Naisi's hand,
Such was the subtlety and valour of the sword.

Feats of the car they showed, Usna's two sons, strange feats
Too long to tell. They took the fancy of the King
So captive by their skill that day, that wild he was
To buy their service. Lands he gave them, broad and fair,
Hunting-lands, pasture-lands : to hold, even to the breast
Of Time Eternal, by the reaping of their swords,
And their sons' swords, in all wars of the King and wars
Of his sons after him. And so they left their dun
And raised on their broad lands a greater dun ; whereto
They came with all their train : their Bard and Harpers three,
War-men, and serving-men, women and household gear,
Horses and hounds. By night they moved, lest prying eye
Should light on Deirdrè's face, and rumour's flying tongue
Stir in the Red King's heart the demons of desire.

THE FIFTH DUAN.

THE FLIGHT FROM ALBA.

So with the Alban King bode Naisi and his Clan,
Doing great deeds of war against his foes. Their fame
Grew loud in all the land ; while Deirdrè in her house
Dwelt with her child, unseen of the wild Alban men.

But on a summer day it chanced she roamed abroad
Into the woods, and sat beneath an oak's huge bole,
With Gaier at her side or playing near ; and mused
On the strange tale of her life : her childhood's lonely days,
Her girlish dreams, her love, her flight from Conchobar ;
Till o'er the happy fields of memory—like the breath
Of Autumn, faint and cold through the glad leaves—there crept

A dim boding of woe, and Cathvah's prophecy,
Long banned, came brooding back—so chill, so full of gloom
It iced the sunniest streams of happy life.   Then first
It shook her soul.   No more the menace of a tale
It seemed, crouching afar for one she never knew,
Some Deirdrè of a dream : she heard the Banshee wail
O'er her own house, and Death drew nigh her in those woods,
She felt his eyes on her, blue, cold, implacable eyes,
Like the eyes of Conchobar, in hatred and desire.

With a low cry : ' Naisi, what have I done to thee ? '
She sprang to snatch her child from where in golden moss
He played, clasping him close with kisses to her breast,
As though to shield him, shield herself, shield all she loved,
In the warm nest of love, from those implacable eyes.

That moment there were eyes indeed in that green wood
Fixt on her, eyes that gazed in wonder on her face,
And felt her beauty smite their vision like the sun,
Painting her image deep in the dark soul of sight ;
For there lurked one who oft, on errands from his lord,
Came prying round the dun, the Steward of the King.
And now his wondering eyes had found Deirdrè ; and fair
She looked that day of the days, under green leaves alone.

Tall was she, like a queen, and graceful as the doe
That hears the hounds' far cry in the green heart of a wood ;
Her standing like a pine shot from the craggy side
Of wild Slieve Mish ; more lithe her bending than the boughs
Of a fair willow, when the whispering summer breeze
Silvers Ard-Sallagh ; sweet the music that she made
In her going, for the eye, as ever for the ear
Of a great King was made by noble harps.   Her face

Was lovelier in its light than the first glorious day
That bares the breast of heaven, and in the o'erwintered grass
Finds the brown lark, and up, shuddering with sudden song,
Lifts him, as with warm kiss upon their crimson lids
It opes the daisies' eyes.   The dewdrops at your feet,
O Deirdrè, were the tears wept by the blissful morn
That looked on you, for joy that it had looked on you !

Blue were her eyes, deep blue as the clear summer sea,
When, murmuring drowsily of isles unknown, it breaks
On the wild western coast : wistful and sad that day !
Deep was the love that dwelt in their blue deeps, and strong
The courage, wise the will, bright in their steadfast fire.
Haws in the morning dew by her fresh lips would seem
A dull half-comely thing to look on.   In her cheek
Glowed the rich blood of health, with crimson fresh and pure
As tinges first the white of ripening strawberries
On a green wood's warm verge.   In the bright coils of her hair
The sunshine, lingering, shed soft splendour in the shade.
O Deirdrè, when the sun shone warm on you that day,
Kissing your shining hair, his warmth was love of you !

Fair from the shoulder gleamed her beautiful white arms,
So soft, so strong, that clasped her strong son to her breast,
That breast superb whereon the champion of the world
Might lay his head unshamed, and dream great dreams.   And there
She stood in her sweet prime, beneath green boughs alone,
The beauty of the world.   O Deirdrè, when the bronze,
Imaging your sweet face, blushed in the light, it blushed
For joy to image you, gazing your beauty back !

The tunic that she wore was yellow as the broom
In morning-light, and wrought with broidered fantasies
The daughters of her hand ; blue was her mantle, hemmed

With silver threads, and brooched with a great brooch of gold
On the left shoulder.   Bare gleamed her two comely arms,
With armlets of soft gold.   The girdle at her waist
Was of dun deerskin, stitched with golden wire, and bossed
With stones in silver set.   On her firm-planted feet
Were hunting buskins, clasped with dainty studs of bronze.
A light sharp hunting-spear, headed with bronze and bright
With rings of silver, lay under the oak ; there too
Her work-bag, and the stuff of wool whereof she wrought
Some garment for the boy, the while she mused cast by.

All this the lurking spy with wonder marked, and thought :
' For this are Usna's Sons the sons of secrecy,
Hiding their houses from us, in the mountain mist !
The sharers of their bread of exile at their board
Are fairy women, stolen out of the haunted hills
Of Ireland.   This is one : some Queen of that old race
Of De Danann, whose name flies on the winds of song
O'er all the world, to vex the heart of men with sighs
For beauty unbeheld.   And I have seen her now ! '

He gazed and gazed again, and even as he gazed,
Seeking to stamp for aye the vision on his brain,
Came Naisi, through the wood striding with eager face ;
And Deirdrè with a cry, love's sunshine in her eyes,
Was in his arms, and close he held her, heart to heart.

Great was the joy between them, and Naisi with his boy
Played like a boy, tossed him with glad shrieks in the air,
Or let his baby hands tug at the magic sword
Of Manannàn.   At last he lifted him aloft,
And on his shoulders bore him laughing from the woods,
Chased by his mother home to their dwelling in the dun.

Then rose the lurking spy, and sped fast to his King,
And watched his hour to say : 'O King of many spoils,
Hidden within their dun the Sons of Usna keep
The glory of the world ! There is no bed of a king
In all the world that holds such beauty as the bed
Of Naisi holds this night. There is no beauty dwells
In women such as dwells in her who lies this night
Beside him. Is it meet the vassal of a King
Should keep for his own joy the jewel that outshines
The treasures of his lord? O, jealous for my King
Were my old eyes this day, first finding their delight !

Then did he paint in words the vision of his mind
So quick with Deirdrè's charms that the Red King took fire,
And cried : 'Ay, Usna's Sons wax high in pride. These Hounds
Of Ulla that I feed will scorn me if they grow
Too lusty for my leash. Bad shows the field of men
Where serfs o'ertop their lords. I'll send this day and take
This woman they have shut from sight in fear of me.'

'Nay,' said the Steward, 'hear, O King of many spoils,
My word of counsel ! Strong are Usna's Sons, and hard
To take in fight the thing they keep. Better their swords
Be for us than against. Cheaper it is to buy
Women with gold than blood ; and dear to women's eyes
Are gold and things of price, jewels and shining robes ;
Dearer to their craving hearts of restless envy all
That clothes in gauds of power their weakness ; and with gold,
And with fair words, may Kings have all their will, and waste
No blood. Leave me to work, and thou shalt have the wife,
Yet keep for thy defence the husband's vassal sword.'

This counsel pleased the King, and with rich gifts of gold
The Steward sought the dun, while Naisi and his Clan
Were on a cattle-spoil abroad, serving the King.
So to the dun he came and found Deirdrè alone.

There in her porch she sat, with Gaier at her side,
And stitched, with loving thoughts, in silken broideries
A little coat.   To her the envoy of the King
Came with a grave salute, gravely returned; and soon
That wily snake, his tongue, creeping in circles fine,
Of flattering talk more near its point of striking, sought
To charm her with its guile.   Deirdrè with hidden fear
Heard him, and guessed some ill, but played with his attack,
Luring him from his lines of ambush craftily.

'Great is your beauty's fame,' he said, 'through all the land.
In vain doth Naisi thus casket in jealous fear
His jewel from the sun.   The birds blab of your face
To the murmuring trees; the streams, whose hidden pools have glassed
Your image, to the meads babble your praise.   Yet he,
Naisi, who keeps you here, mewed from the world that wakes
But for your worship, Naisi, he can forget your face,
Even as the wanton bee forgets the queen of the woods
That holds the richest sweets, for meaner flowers agape
To every thirsty fly—Naisi—'
                                    With flashing eyes
She cried, 'What means this talk of Naisi?'   'By your leave,
I will be plain,' he said.   'You pine here in your dun
Beyond the rim of the world, or you would know how lives
Your Naisi in the world.   The grey chief of Duntroon
Has a fair daughter—sweet the secrets that she kept
Till Naisi came.   He wooed the kisses of her mouth
With a shy doe of the woods, blithe with her frisking fawn,
When back from Inverness he came last year.'   She smiled,

In pale disdain, and said : ' Beware, lest for this tale
I give thy wagging tongue such guerdon as befits
The slanderous makebate.   Hence !   When wives are loyal, fool,
They have no ears to hear the secrets of their lord,
Save from his lips alone.   While go thou mayest, begone ! '

Wondering he bowed ; yet stayed, still trusting his grey craft
To mesh the veering mind of woman in his net,
Woven out of jealous wrath, vexed pride, pleased vanity ;
And, flattering still, he flashed the jewels in her eyes,
And laid them in her lap, with pleading for his King.

But Deirdrè rose in wrath, and cried with a stern cry,
' To my side, Clan Usna ! '   Straight Ardàn, left in the dun
Her guard, was at her side.   Then, with a scorn that made
Each word a whip, she said : ' Black be the day, O son
Of a bad mother, black the day that first mine eyes
Looked on thy traitor face !   And black for thee shall be
The day that mine thou sawest.   O wretch, know that my name
Is Deirdrè, and to thee dreadful shall be the sound !
This answer take thy King ! '   And with the word she spat
Upon the gifts of gold, and in the Steward's face
So fiercely flung them, back he staggered from the blow,
Stunned, bleeding, scared, and turned to fly.   Fierce to Ardàn :
' Slay me this dog ! ' she cried.   ' He comes with his vile dross
To buy me for his lord.'   Ardàn with one swift stroke
Smote him.   The headless trunk fell prone, the severed head
Beside it, in the dust puddled with blood.   A shriek
From frighted women rose ; and Gaier, who had stood
Grasping his mother's gown, set up a startled cry.

Deirdrè upon her breast soothed him ; then stern and pale
Stept with him to the corse, which lay as it had fallen,
A grovelling heap.   ' Come boy,' she said, ' the sons of kings
Must early learn to look upon a foe struck dead.'

They cast the body forth beyond the dun, and strewed
Fresh earth upon the blood.   The gory head they laid,
With all the golden heap of treasure, on a bench
Within the House of Arms, to wait Naisi's award.

Next day came Naisi back with all his Clan.   The tale
He heard.   Fierce burnt his wrath against the treacherous King.
'We have no more a home,' he said.   'The Swans of Lir
Call to us o'er the waves to seek another shore.
The western sea has isles beloved of Manannàn,
To them shall be our flight.   Farewell to the broad fields
Our swords have won !   Farewell to the comrades we have pledged!
When friends turn foes, farewell the halls of revelry !
Welcome the lonely shores where mourn the Swans of Lir !'

That night they sent away their women from the dun
Back to where still the ships, beached by their trusty crews,
Lay hid for use at need.   Ardàn with fifty spears
Led them by secret ways down to the firth, and gave
Command to make all trim for sea.   The bustling crews
Leaped blithely at his word, and by the morrow's noon
The galleys, tight and trim, rode on the silver flood,
Like sea-birds ere they spread their wings for southward flight.

And that same night was flung into the King's great dun,
Wrapt in a broidered scarf, the Steward's gory head ;
Its chill hair decked with gold and jewels—all the gifts
To Deirdrè from the King.   And with it was this rann :
    'This head of the King's man, slain by their hands, with gold
    In eric for his death, the Sons of Usna send.
    His body lies the while unburied by their dun,
    Let the King claim it there, his claim shall be allowed.'

Thereat the Red King's face was changed with fury.   He raged
Like one gone suddenly mad.   With cruel foot he spurned
His hound best loved, the gift of Naisi, when she came
Perplexed, with fawning whine, to lick his wrathful hand,
So sorely that the beast fled howling from the hall.

Anon he gave command to arm in haste ; but first
Sent on a deft slinger, to sling into the hold
Of Usna's Sons this rann, tied to a whizzing stone :
　'No eric will I take, save this : three heads for one,
　Till this I come to take abide me, if ye dare.'

This message Naisi found ere noon, close to the door
Of Deirdrè's house.   The stone had struck the painted post
And left it scarred.   The song of battle in his heart,
Rose as he cried aloud : 'He answers like a King.
Well, he shall have our heads, let him but win them now !'

To Ainli then he spoke : 'Against this dun of ours
The Red King comes to-day, to take our heads.   Our craft
Must draw him to the glens, where, while we seem to fly,
We shall fight, flying.   There !' he pointed to a gorge
Scarring the mountain side.   'There shall we make our stand,
In yonder pass, whereof each bush and rock we know
Blindfolded in the night.   Brother of all my deeds,
To thee this day I yield the post of valour.   Choose
Three score, the Clan's best men, skilled with the sling, the spear,
The sword, not scant of breath, stags of the mountain, strong
To breast the craggy scaurs without a sob.   With these
Here thou shalt hold the dun against the King's assault,
Then burst away to me, luring him to the pass
Where I with all my power will spring upon his rout.'

Joy shone in Ainli's eyes. 'Thanks, brother, for this boon.
This will I do, or know what death men die, when swords
Reap them in the red van of onset.   Many a field
Has known me for a stout reaper ; and when in turn
Among the sheaves of war I lie, to rush no more
Through bleeding ranks, comely shall be the sheaves that day,
Comely my wounds shall be, comely the trampled grass
That drinks my blood.   But now have thou no fear for me :
I think we shall not die to-day.   Many a shrewd hour
Of peril have we shared, Ardan and thou and I,
Since with Cuchullin first we learned all feats of war
From red-maned Scatha.   Here in Alba none shall say
We shamed her school.   Farewell ! ' With a grave look of love
The brothers kissed ; then turned to order their array.

Soon Ainli picked his men, and Naisi with his band
Marched from the dun, and up the mountain-side, away
To the wild gorge ; waving, before they passed from sight
A last farewell to that bold few keeping the dun.

Not long had these to wait for the Red King ; for soon
Far down the valley rose the sound of coming war :
The bag-pipe's eager scream, shrill o'er the brazen roar
Of war-horns braying loud as furious bulls, was heard,
First faintly, then more near ; till, as the sturdy van
Of gold-bought Norsemen came in view, the mountains round
Seemed roaring to the noise of airy hosts, so loud
Echoed the crags.   Meanwhile the dun upon its hill,
Answering with silence, loomed stern as the bolted cloud
Which speaks not ere it strike.   Behind their wattled walls
Hidden the Irish lay, while Ainli through a loop
Marked with a wary eye the coming of the King.

And soon, like the first dash of thunder-driven hail,
The slingers' volleyed stones came singing o'er the dun,
Rattling on every roof and wooden shed.   No shout
Or stir of men made answer, till, even as the King
Halted to form his ranks for the assault, out rang
Ainli's shrill whistle ; then, swift leaping to their mounds
With a wild cry, the slingers plied their Irish slings
With springy staves of yew.   Keen was their instant aim,
Deadly the stones they sent'from staves well-bent that day,
Hissing like snakes of the air.   The stone from Ainli's hand
Smote the King's crest, and shore his griffin's golden wing ;
And many a man fell slain.   Seven times the Irish leaped
And slang, and bent their heads reloading, ere the van
Of Alba rushing came to scale the dun, and fierce,
Spear to spear, axe to axe, they grappled at the fosse.

But when the King's wild horde with axes hewed their way
Through the tough wattled walls, or vaulting with their spears
Leaped over them to death, Ainli, with scarce a man
Hard hit or slain outright, with axes and great spears
Charged from the rearward gate, and through the thronging foe,
Like a tall herd of elks dashing with gory horns
The yelling pack aside, made desperate way, and sought
With swift and sudden rush the safety of the hills.

Then was a noble race ; for, straining after them,
The Red King urged the chase.   There Ainli, Swift of Foot,
Shewed him new deeds of war, as up the mountain-side,
Easily as o'er the plain, he sped, drawing as he ran
The swiftest in pursuit, then, fiercely turning, slew
With sword or spear ; and so, still fighting, fled the band.

And still the stubborn King upon their bloody track
Urged on his labouring van, past many a gory corse
Of their slain comrades, still by Ainli's craft led on,
The quarry full in view.   Thus for an hour they toiled
Up the steep mountain-side, until the Irish won
The gorge's gripe, and stood.   On came the raging King
With all his force, in haste to glut his baffled rage.

But Ainli whistled shrill, mocking the curlew's cry;
And straightway down the rocks burst Naisi and his men
In three swift streams, leaping like brooks in sudden storm
Upon the wearied foe, clogged by their numbers.   Loud
Rang the wild din of war through the thronged pass, and well
Fought the Red King.   An axe with his long arms he swayed,
And where it fell helms cracked and heads of men went down.

Him Naisi marked afar, and challenged with a shout;
And through the battle-press the two, like charging bulls
That cleave with eager fronts the scattering herds between,
Made at each other : red the lanes they hewed that day,
Ere face to face they met.   Like sundered herds the clans
Shrank from their battle-ground.   Never came death more near
Naisi; for the tough King smote like a sturdy smith
Great blows and swift, and like an eagle his huge axe
Struck on the swoop, and soared again without a pause.

But Naisi, leaping back, gave ground, and drew the King
About the field, and still upon the axe's haft
Smote with his sword's keen edge.   Three blows he struck, the third
Left the axe headless.   Then he waited till the King
His buckler snatched, and drew the sword upon his thigh,
And lashed at him in rage.   His shield baffled the blow;
Then fiercely, blade to blade and shield to shield, they closed
In furious fight.   Shrill sang their swords, their dinted shields

Cried hoarsely o'er the din of war, and grisly wounds
They gave and took; till soon from arms bleeding and faint
Drooped their hacked shields. But now pressed Naisi on the King,
Driving him foot by foot backwards, till with a leap
Full on his helm he smote. The sword of Manannàn,
Cleaving the crest, cut through the scalp, and bit the bone.
He fell, and over him Naisi, his victor's foot
Planted upon his neck, stood with his bloody sword
Poised like a hovering hawk. 'O King,' he said, 'my hand
Henceforth might wear for thee the ring of gold which decks
The slayer of a King! Yet keep thy life. Two years
Thy wage have Usna's Sons taken, and shared thy bread,
To-day's shame pays enough thy guile to us. Farewell,
Haply thou shalt see fly thy fortune with our swords!'

At the King's fall his host fled in dismay, pursued
With havoc down the pass; till Naisi's clarion blew.
The wounded King he gave into his henchman's hand,
To bear from that red field. The Brothers with their Clan,
Many slain, many hurt, marched from their victory
By sunset to their ships, where Deirdrè hailed with joy
Naisi and Ainli safe. With gentle surgery
She bathed and bound their wounds, smiling in sweet content
To hear their warrior's tale of peril scaped that day.

At dawn they rowed from shore, then hoisted sail, and passed
By many an isle and sound, voyaging by day, by night
Anchoring in land-locked bays, or, with ships hauled ashore,
Resting on lonely strands; so seven long days they sailed,
Till by Loch Eta's mouth a goodly isle they found
Where no man dwelt, pleasant with forest-land, and good
For hunters. There they made a year their quiet home.

THE SIXTH DUAN.

THE PLEDGE OF FERGUS.

Meanwhile to Erin came tiding of all the deeds
By Usna's exiled Sons in Alba done.   Their tale,
Roaming about the land in songs of wandering Bards,
Wrought woe in the Red Branch, and murmurs through the halls
Of Eman darkly crept from mouth to mouth.   Men said :
' Bad is their banishment for a frail woman's fault,
Great our loss, losing them.   Better, if die they must
For slight of Conchobar, by us their heads should fall
In their own land, than thus to bring disgrace upon us
Banished and foully slain, haply, by hands unknown.'

These murmurs to the ear of Conchobar crept on
By crooked ways ; for none, fearing his eye, durst name
The name of Usna's Sons.   In his fierce heart fierce love,
Stung by the scorn of a girl, pent like a caverned plague,
Sat brooding, bayed about with evil dreams.   And now
Like a thawed snake it stirred.   Like wolves whimpering for blood
Cruel desires, dark thoughts, hunted about his brain
The phantoms of his foes, and smarting shame, arrayed
In Kingship's flouted robe, ever hounded them on.

So the long-dreamed-of hour drew near.   There was a feast
Held in the Red Branch House ; and bidden to that feast
Came all the Red Branch chiefs ; and over their high seats,
Ranged in precedence due, the heralds hung their shields,
Summoning with trumpet-blasts the Orders, rank by rank.
There, with the Kings and Chiefs, came Druids old in fame,

Ollavs and Shanachies, Harpers and Bards, the best
That sang within the ring of the four circling seas ;
And well they cheered that feast, chanting the deeds of yore ;
And well they sang the growth of Trees of Ancestry,
Branches of Kingship, grafts of high alliance—all
The lore of Houses, Clans and Septs ; fair births, brave deaths :
All that sustains the pride and glory of great Kings.

But when the royal feast's loud mirth was full in flood
Shancha the Ollav rose, and took his golden Branch
Of Music in his hand ; and from its tuneful bells
Shook silence, like soft dew, on the long table's roar,
Stilling the jester's tongue.   Then thrice a henchman smote
The silver sounding-dish hung from the canopy
Of the King's chair of state ; and like the ocean's voice
Hushing the streams was heard the voice of Conchobar.

He sent into the air his kingly voice, and awe
Rode on the sound of it.   ' O warrior Kings ! ' he said,
' Is there in all the world a better house than this
For all good cheer and mirth, and pleasant speech of friends ? '
' Not one ! ' they said.   ' Ye know no want then, feel no lack
For any pleasant thing to season this high feast ? '
' None, none ! ' they cried again.   Then with a sigh the King
Said sadly : ' 'Tis not so with me : one want I know
That ever sours for me the choicest sweets of mirth.
Where are old Usna's Sons this day ?   Where is the joy
Of any feast without them ?   Sad are the songs we make,
Wanting their voices ; blank the walls we deck with shields,
Wanting their shields.   No tune lives in the golden tongue
Of any Bard for me ; no music in the strings
Of sweet three-cornered harps.   To me the noble voice
Of gallant hounds that snuff the dew of the morn is sad

G

As the ill-omened howl of watch-dogs in the night ;
Sad is the sun himself till next I see his beam
Shine on three heads not here.   Usna's three Sons should sit,
Kings among Kings ; and now they wander far and wide
In lonely lands, alone.   A woman is the cause—
A bad cause ; for I think no woman ever born
Were worth so dear a loss.   Shall we not have them home ? '

Glad was the whole Red Branch to hear him speak this word.
' O Conchobar,' they said, ' the rivers of thy tongue
Have swept our hidden thoughts this hour into the light.
But who shall bring them back, seeing their oath is on them
Ne'er to return, until, in surety for their lives,
Be pledged Cormac, thy son, Cuchullin, Fergus Roy,
Or Conall Carnach ? '   ' Well,' said Conchobar, ' be it so ;
But have them back we will.'   Then with new joy the feast
Grew loud once more, and song rose in the Red-Branch House.

Next morning, ere the dew was dried upon the grass,
About his orchard long paced Conchobar alone,
Brooding.   ' Now will I try their hearts,' he thought, ' now prove
Who loves me best.'   And soon he found an hour to speak
With Conall secretly.   ' O warrior King ! ' he said,
' Comrade of many deeds, I know thou lov'st me well ;
As thou hast cause, for twice my arm has kept thy head.
Tell me : what wouldst thou do if I should send thee now
For Usna's Sons, and death perchance should come to them
Under thy surety ? '   ' This,' said Conall, ' and no worse :
Not one man's life alone should pay me for their lives,
But every treacherous heart that should abet their death
Would I tear out.'   Fiercely his two terrible eyes,
The blue eye and the brown, flamed on the King, who turned
His darkened face away, muttering : ' Henceforth I know
Thou lov'st me not.'   And so dealt Conall with the King.

Next, in a chosen hour, he drew Cuchullin to him,
And said: 'O warrior King, I know thou lov'st me well,
Being my sister's son; and I it was, thou knowest,
Who gave thee thy first spears.   When thou wast but a boy
I made thee Champion, gave thee my own car and my steeds,
And made with noble arms noble thy untried hand,
And, in the paths of fame planting thy feet, set foes
Before thy beardless face.   Tell me, my son, if now
I pledge thee to bring back the Sons of Usna safe,
And by ill-hap some hurt should light upon their heads,
What wouldst thou do?'   'But this,' Cuchullin said, 'no more,
And by my sword, no less!   If wrong should come to them
I would not take from thee the riches of the East—
The bribe of all the world; but thou and all thy clan
Should pay me with your heads for the blackness of your hearts.
Strong are the ties of blood, but stronger for good men
The ties of honour.'   Fierce the flame of his blue eyes
Blazed on the King's dark face.   'Well said!' quoth Conchobar,
'I see thou lov'st me not.'   He turned his back, and strode
Angry away.   So dealt Cuchullin with the King.

He came to Fergus.   'Thou,' he said, 'O warrior King,
Father of my renown! if I should send thee now
To bring back Usna's Sons in peace, and by ill-chance
Some hurt should come to them under thy surety, tell me,
What wouldst thou do?'   Then laughed Fergus a careless laugh,
'What evil chance could come to any man brought back
Under my pledge?   If aught save good should come to them
Woe to the man whose mind should compass their mishap;
His head should fall by me, save thine alone, my son.'
'Well hast thou spoken, friend,' said Conchobar.   'Go thou
To where in lone Loch Eta, in an isle of the sea
The Sons of Usna dwell.   Go, bring them back in peace,
And with their longed-for sight comfort our broken Branch!'

Then Conchobar was glad, and straightway to the North
To Barach in his dun, hard by the port that looks
Towards Alba, o'er the strait where once the Swans of Lir
Mourned for three hundred years on the chill tides of Moyle,
Sent by sure hands this word : 'Barach, thou knowest me well,
My favour and my wrath.   Now therefore, on thy life,
Do this my bidding : watch for Fergus when he comes
From Alba, bringing safe the Sons of Usna home,
And meet him when he lands, and bid him on his vow
Ne'er to refuse a feast, unto a seven days' feast
Within thy house.   Do this, and hold him to his vow,
Or headless thou shalt find thy sons, left in my hand.'

But in his galley sailed Fergus without a host,
And with him went his sons, two youths, Illàn the Fair,
Buiné the Ruthless Red ; and with him went beside
Callan his shield-bearer, bearing his mighty shield ;
And swiftly sailed his ship, and came ere many days
To where in Eta Loch the Sons of Usna lay.

There in this wise they dwelt : they had built three booths of chase,
In one they cooked, in one they fed, and in the third
They slept.   When Fergus marked these booths far-off, his heart
Leaped in him, for the love of Usna's noble Sons.
Gladly he brought them peace.   Great was the shout that came
Out of his throat that day ; for noble was his voice
In shouting, over all the voices of the men
Of Ulla.   Great and glad it sounded in the glens
Of Eta, like the shout of a mighty man of chase
Who sees his quarry ; far it rang through Naisi's isle,
A noble shout and loud, no treachery in its tone.

Now Naisi in the booth with Deirdrè sat, and there
Between them open lay the board of Conchobar,
' *Fairhead*,' his trothal-gift to Deirdrè, and thereon
They played at chess.   And when the voice of Fergus came
To Naisi's ear, he sprang straight to his feet and said :
' Surely I heard the cry of a man of Eri ! '   ' Nay,'
Said Deirdrè, ' bad the ear that hears an Irish cry
Come from an Alban throat.   Play on ! '   But sudden dread
Had clutched her heart, when first she heard the pealing voice
Of Fergus.   Nearer then there came a second cry,
And Naisi said : ' No man of Alba, but a man
Of Eri gave that shout.'   ' No, no,' said Deirdrè.   ' Come,
Play ! play ! '   Then Fergus drew nearer the booths, and gave
A third right hearty cheer.   And surely knew the Sons
Of Usna who came there ; and Naisi said : ' Go thou,
Ardàn, and greet Fergus, and bring him in to us.'

But Deirdrè wrung her hands, sighing deeply, and said :
' Ochone ! too well I guessed whose voice gave that first shout—
Fergus Mac Roy, ochone ! Fergus Mac Roy, I knew him
Too well, too well ! '   ' But why,' said Naisi, ' girl of my heart,
Didst thou hide this from me ? '   ' Last night,' said she, ' I dreamed,
And in my dream there flew three birds into our bed,
In their three beaks three drops of honey, and they left
The honey on my lips, but drank from me instead
Three drops of my heart's blood.'   ' What means this dream of
    thine ? '
Said he.   She answered, ' Sweet as honey on the lips
Is a false man's false word of peace to us this day ;
And those three drops of blood the birds drank from my breast,
What are they but your lives stol'n from me, stol'n this day
By Conchobar's false words ?   For well I know that naught
Will stay you ; ye will go with Fergus to your doom,
Will go to Conchobar, beguiled, beguiled, beguiled ! '

Her words dismayed them all ; but Naisi said : ' Let come
What will come, Fergus waits upon us.   Go to him,
Ardàn, and greet him well, and bring him hither straight,
Were it my death, I long to see an Irish face.'

Then went Ardàn and greeted Fergus and his sons,
And gave them lovingly three kisses on the face,
And brought them to the booth.   There Naisi made great cheer
To see them, and he kissed Fergus right fervently
And many times, and kissed his sons ; and so likewise
Did Deirdrè, and greeting each in turn welcomed them all.

And Naisi asked for tales of Eman, and of all
The doings of the Branch.   ' This is the happiest tale,'
Said Fergus, ' that we come from Conchobar to you,
To bring you peace ; in pledge whereof I stand this day
Your surety, sworn and bound.   And ever, as ye know,
I have been dear to you, and loved you, and my vow
Is on me to fulfil my warranty this day.
Under me ye were lost, with me ye shall go home.'

Deep Naisi sighed thereat.   ' Ay, that is truth,' said he.
' This is a goodly land, but not my land.   Not here
Our mother kissed us first ; not here our father saw
His boys grow strong ; not here our kinsmen's cairns are green ;
Though great our having here, 'tis Ireland has my love.
Fair be her fortunes !   O, the fields my childhood knew,
The flowers upon her fields, the fair skies over them !
White were the daisies there in springtime in her fields,
Yellow the cowslips there, yellow upon her hills
The scented furze, and blue the bluebells of her woods !
Sweet in the autumn there the apples that we plucked,

I and my brothers, sweet the first-found blackberries
Riping on the hot rocks! O for the thrush's note
In her glad woods first heard, the blackbird's whistle there!
O the red stags of her glens, the eagles of her crags,
That first I climbed; and O, the first brave hounds I followed
Through the sweet Irish dew! I left my life behind
When I left Ireland. O, the comrades that I had
In Ireland! O, the games on Eman's Green, the feasts
In the Red Branch House, the friendly faces in the hall,
Irish and true! My heart, a bird above the waves,
Flies to the glad green fields of Ireland, that I love:
I am a lonely man till I am home in Ulla!'

'Till then will not be long,' said Fergus, 'if ye trust
My word and warranty.' 'We trust them, as we trust
The sun to rise by day,' said Naisi, 'and with thee
Will we go back, and fear no spleen of Conchobar.'

But Deirdrè had no part in Naisi's words, and hung
Weeping about his neck: 'Home, home!' she said. 'What home
Have I where thou art not? Thou art the nest of love
Where my heart folds its wings in peace. Here is my home;
For here I have thee safe. Ireland lies whelmed below
Grey treacherous seas. No home can I have there; for there
They will take thee from me—O, go not with Fergus there!
For my sake, for thy boy's, go not to Conchobar!'

But Fergus answered her gently: 'Hold not thy lord,
O Deirdrè, from his fame; for what praise shall he have
In this wild isle of the sea? But in the Red Branch House
Like music shall his name sound on the golden tongue
Of noble Bards. Let fear die in thy breast. My shield
Is over you, the shield of Fergus. Let the men

Of Ulla all turn false, and seek your death, Fergus
Will not be false.   My sword, and my sons' swords alone
Could hold you harmless, came the quarters of the world
In arms against us three.'   But Deirdrè sighed : 'Ay, Fergus,
The craft of Conchobar has made thy honesty
A fair mouth to persuade Naisi into his net.'

'The lie ne'er stained his tongue,' said Naisi, 'and with him
Will I go back.   My feet are sore for Eman's Green ;
Minè eyes are sore to see the Red Branch House, my friends,
The comrades of my deeds ; so let who loves me now
Follow me o'er the seas.   With Fergus I will go.'

They bore away that night, under a moon that made
The sea a silver lake of glory, and the isles
Loom huge as dusky cairns of sea-kings.   Naisi sat
With Fergus on the poop, talking of days of yore ;
But Deirdrè in her cloak lay still and spoke no word,
Clasping her child to her breast from the cold wind of the sea ;
Till the bright moon sank low, and in the east the stars
Last risen paled, feeling the pallid eyes of dawn.

There in the dawn they heard from the high fields of air
Music on downy wing come floating—magical
Sweet fairy music, sad as the lone wind of the sea
Makes evermore at dawn, answering the homeless waves.
It was the Swans of Lir, to the wild West away
Flying in sorrow back from the ruined halls of Lir.

And Deirdrè in the dawn arose, and on the poop
Sat down, pale as the dawn, and gazed back to the coast
Of Alba ; and the Swans' wild dirge stirred in her heart
Dirges for her own sorrow ; and she sang this lay :

DEIRDRÈ'S FAREWELL TO ALBA.

1.

O Land, Land of my heart,
There sinks my joy in the waters!
O Alba ne'er would I leave thee,
But now I go with my lover!

2.

I waft farewell o'er the waters
To you, Dun-finn and Dun-fiagh,
My love to the hills above you,
My love to the Isle of Drayno!

3.

O wood of Cone, green wood
Where Ainli roved in the morning,
Too short the days that I sigh for,
No more in Alba with Naisi!

4.

Glen of Laith, Glen of Laith,
Where warm I slept in thy covert,
On badger's brawn and on venison
You feasted me, Glen of Laith!

5.

Glen Masàn, Glen Masàn,
Long grow the leaves of thy hart's-tongues;
But never more shall ye rock me,
O grassy creeks of Masàn!

6.

But thou, Glen Eta, Glen Eta,
Where first I ordered my homestead,
O happy thou madst my rising,
Sweet nook of the sun, Glen Eta!

7.

Glen of the Roes, Glen-da-Rua,
Blest be the man who loves thee!
Sweet shouts over bending branches
The cuckoo in Glen-da-Rua!

8.

O Drayno of sounding shore,
White gleams the sand through thy water,
Dear Drayno, ne'er would I leave thee,
But now I go with my lover!

Well sailed the swift war-ship, the 'Courser of the Seas,'
With Deirdrè and the Chiefs; and soon they made a port
Of Ireland; and anon they came to Barach's dun.
There Barach welcomed them, kissing with kisses three
The Sons of Usna; and made fair welcome with his lips
To Fergus and his Sons; but guile hid in his heart.
'O Fergus, I have here a feast for thee!' he said,
'Here bide thou shalt seven days; for in thy vows it is
Ne'er to refuse a feast, nor leave the house of mirth
Till all be ended. Come, seven days thou art my guest,
And never stepped a man more welcome through my door.'

Then Fergus groaned in wrath and anguish, and his face
And all his body burnt, one crimson fire of shame.
'Evil is this thou hast done, O Barach, laying thus
My vow upon me! Well thou knowest that Conchobar
Has bound me with an oath to bring him, that same day
We touch the Irish coast, the Sons of Usna safe.'

But Barach smiling said: 'What other vows thou hast
I know not. This I know: if thou refuse this feast
My mouth will spit such shame upon thee from this day
Till thy death-day as never champion should endure.'

And Fergus, with bowed head, to Naisi turned, and sighed :
' What shall I do ? '   Deirdrè in rage and scorn burst out :
' Go to this feast, hang up our safety with thy shield
In Barach's house, lay by the sword of our defence !
Go, feast upon our flesh, and drink our blood with him !
Black is the tongue that bade thee, black as his beetle heart ;
Go thou, fulfil thy vow, forsake us for a feast ! '

' Nay, I forsake you not,' said Fergus, ' on my head
Be still your safety.   Here I give you my two sons,
To bring you on your way, under my pledge ; and came
The five great fifths of all Ireland in arms, to break
That safeguard, have no fear ; for it should not be broke.'

' Enough,' said Naisi, ' be our safeguard our own swords,
They never failed us yet.'   In wrath he strode away,
Bade Fergus no farewell, turning for no last look
On his old friend, and so saw him no more.   The rest
Followed him.   Fergus, left in Barach's dun behind,
Gazed after them, the light of his fresh sunny face
Quenched in a darkening cloud of sorrow.   His two sons
Kissed him in haste, and went the way of many feet.

But, as in wrath and gloom they took the nearest way
To Eman, ' Will ye hear my counsel ? ' Deirdrè said ;
Though, to your loss, I know ye hold me little wise ? '
' What counsel, girl of my heart ? ' said Naisi.   ' Speak thy mind.'
' Then seek awhile,' she said, ' the safety of the sea ;
Turn back with me to-night, and let your galley steer
To Inish Cullen.   There, between the land and the land,
Let us four dwell awhile, till Fergus eat his fill
Of Barach's bloody feast.   Let him fulfil his vow,
Yet keep his troth.   Turn back—long life and happy days
Call you upon my tongue, will ye but hear me now ! '

But Naisi frowned and said : ' Nay, where my right foot goes
My left foot follows.   On ! for death met face to face
Smites a fair champion's blow ; but shunned skulks like a thief
With skene-wounds for the back.   Danger is dangerous most
When men turn back, and find wisdom in woman's fears.'

The Sons of Fergus too were grieved at Deirdrè's words,
And said : ' Woman, whose face is fairer on the earth
Than the sun's face in heaven, thine is an evil mind
For us, dishonouring so the keeping of our swords ;
For, were there not the might of your own hands with ours,
The word of Fergus holds : ye shall not be betrayed.'

But Deirdrè sighed, and said : ' Woe met me in that word
In Alba, woe drew near when Fergus, breaking troth,
Forsook us for a feast.'   And on her way she went
Greatly cast down, and made even as she went this lay :

DEIRDRÈ'S COMPLAINT OF FERGUS

1.

Bitter, bitter is my heart
This day, for the word of Fergus ;
I go not back from my saying :
Woe came with the word of Fergus.

2

A clot of woe is my heart
This day for the Sons of Usna,
Chill dawns your death-day upon me
Ye comely Children of Usna !

3.

In Alba the red stag roams,
But gone are the Sons of Usna ;
Ochone ! a ship was my sorrow,
Long, long the day of my grieving !

So on they fared, and came to the watch-tower of Fincarn ;
But Deirdrè in the glen loitered for heaviness ;
And sleep fell on her there ; and, knowing not her case,
They left her in the glen, till Naisi, missing her,
Turned back and found her there, alone in the wild glen,
Rising from sleep.   And pale she stared on him, and wild
Her eyes were, as the eyes of a young doe that hears,
Deep in the dewy fern, at dawn, the hounds' first bay.

He caught her in his arms : 'Why tarriest thou, my Queen,
In this lone spot?' he said.   And she : 'Sleep, sleep upon me,
And in that sleep a dream, and in that dream a sight—
A woeful sight I have seen : Usna's three Sons, you three,
Bloody on the cold grass, without your heads ; there too
Illàn the Fair, your help headless in him ; and one
That kept his head, well-named "the Ruthless," and in him
No help, but treachery, treachery in him who kept his head ! '

Thereafter on they went, and came at set of sun
To Ard-na-Sallagh.   There Deirdrè beheld a cloud
Crimson like blood, and said : ' O Naisi, mark that cloud !
It is thy cloud.   And blood is in that cloud, thy blood,
Ready to fall.   O, now take safety from the tongue
Of my last counsel !   Hear, hear me, ye noble Sons
Of Usna ! Let me speak!' 'What wouldst thou have?' said they.

' Turn ye this night aside,' she said, ' and take the way
Unto Dundalgan.   There Cuchullin lies, there bide
Till Fergus come ; or go, under Cuchullin's pledge,
To Eman -Macha.' 'Nay,' said Naisi, ' Wilt thou quell
Our souls with woman's fear ?'   Then Deirdrè sang this lay :

DEIRDRÈ'S PLEADING.

1.

Look on thy cloud, O Naisi !
Over the west where it hovers,
Over the Green of Eman,
Is horror of blood, O Naisi !

2.

It lifts the hair on my forehead,
It crisps the skin of my bosom ;
For like the clot of thy heart-vein
Is that thin cloud, O Naisi !

3.

Ah ! never before, ah ! never
Came parting of ways between us,
Our tongues were both in one story,
Thy tongue and mine, O Naisi !

4.

Together in joy and sorrow
We roamed the land and the waters ;
But never, by land or water,
Wast thou against me, O Naisi !

5.

But now, O Lord of my longing !
Thy frown chides darkly my pleading :
O never till now in counsel
Wast thou against me, O Naisi !

And after that they went, still by the shortest way,
Till Eman Macha lay before them, nothing changed :
They seemed to have shut their eyes an hour, and dreamed a dream
Of exile, and awaked ; and there it stood unchanged
As were the ancient hills.   Three warrior shouts they gave
Of greeting to the dun and Eman's pleasant Green.

'A sign,' said Deirdrè then, 'I give you, that will show
The mind of Conchobar, whether he means you well,
Or broods on treachery now.'   'What is that sign ?' said they.
'If to the Red-Branch House he sends you with fair words,
Yet sees you not, the mind is false in him this night.'

To Conchobar's High House they came, and on the door
Knocked with the handwood.   'Ho !' the door-ward from within
Cried to them : 'Who are ye ?'   'The Sons of Usna, come
In peace to Conchobar, with Deirdrè, and the Sons
Of Fergus.'   And that news he brought to Conchobar.

'How is the Red Branch House,' said Conchobar, 'for meat ?
For drink, and all good cheer fitting the noblest guests ?'
And it was told him : 'Came all the seven hosts at once
Out of all Ulster, there they might lie down, and taste
The abundance of the realm.'   'A good word is that word,'
Said Conchobar.   'Bring there the Sons of Usna straight,
And feast them well on all the abundance of the realm.'

Then came the door-ward back, welcoming them all by name,
And told them.   'Ah, Naisi !' said Deirdrè, 'to thy. hurt
Thou hast scorned my counsel—come, depart and keep your lives,
While ye have lives to keep.   Bide ye this night at least
With Conall Carnach safe.   Dunseverick is not far.'

But Buinè said : 'Not so.   There has not yet been found
The coward's face on us, nor the unmanly mind ;
These are but woman's fears.   On to the Red-Branch House !'
So to the Red-Branch House they came, that night to abide.

THE SEVENTH DUAN.

THE RED BRANCH HOUSE.

There bode they in the House of the Red-Branch, and well
The servants of the King welcomed them.   On the board
All kinds of noble food, served for the honoured guests
Of a great king, they spread before them : savoury meats,
And mighty horns of ale, and cups of gold afoam
With strong nut-coloured mead.   And all their folk were glad
And feasted, and forgot the weariness of the way.

But Deirdrè with the Sons of Usna sat apart
In wrath, and would not eat ; and Naisi bade one bring
' *Fairhead*,' the royal board, the gift of Conchobar,
Inlaid with mother-of-pearl, and gold, and ivory ;
Its men, of sea-horse tooth and agate, set with gems.
This board they brought, and ranged the pieces in array
For Naisi and his Queen ; and there they played at chess,
Deirdrè and Naisi.   And all their folk, feasting, drank deep.

Meanwhile the king's proud heart wrought like an eager tide
Vext by an adverse wind in a deep strait.   He longed
To see once more the face of Deirdrè ; for her voice
Was murmuring in his ear like a remembered tune,
And like a ghost her form seemed ever gliding near,
But a half-luminous cloud was ever on the face.

Anon he cried aloud : ' O warriors, which of you
Will bring me faithful word if Deirdrè keep the form
She had when last in love I looked upon her face ?
Keep she it still, no woman born of a woman breathes

Whose form would, set by hers, not seem but mire to gold.'
Then Lavarcam, long since crept back to her old place
By the King's ear, burst out : ' I claim that service, King !
None else shall go, myself will bring thee tiding true.'

Now thus it was with her, the gossip Lavarcam :
Naisi she loved beyond all men upon the earth,
And would have run the round of all the world, to taste
One kiss of his mouth ; and Deirdrè, her child, she loved beyond
The tongue of Bards to tell.   She would have given the drops
From her heart's vein to cure her child of any woe,
Counting it her good luck.   So to the Red-Branch House,
At Conchobar's behest, she ran with eager feet.

There found she whom she sought, ' *Fairhead* ' between the two,
And they two playing thereon.   There in her aged hands
She took their heads beloved, and rained upon their cheeks,
And lips, and eyes, kisses—kisses of loyalty,
Kisses of love ; and there her tears ran down like rain
Suddenly loosed from heaven, till all her breast was wet
With the rivers of her love, gushed forth to welcome them.

' O children of my heart ! ' she sighed.   ' How have ye fared
This many a day ?   Ochone ! it is not well this night,
Not well for you to have between you there that thing
He was most loath to lose, next to yourself, my lamb,
Next to yourself, my girl !   And ye here in his power,
Whom he most hates !   And now, know ye why I am here ?
I am sent to see if still my Deirdrè keep the form
She had upon her once ; but I'll tear out my tongue
Ere what my old eyes have seen I tell to Conchobar :
The form upon her then was, to the form that shines
Upon her now, but as the beauty of a child

H

To the beauty of a Queen!   Ah! why, pulse of my heart—
Ah! why, pearl of my life, art thou come here to fill
Conchobar's veins with fire?   O, never till this night
I knew what beauty was!   What blame should any man,
Much less a mighty King, have, though he gave the fish
Of the nine rivers blood for water, for thy sake?'

'O sad, sad is my soul for the deed they plot this night,
My jewels, against you all; for treachery and shame
And troth-break are this night come near to Conchobar.
And after this bad night will Eman never know
Any good hour again.'   Wherefore she made this lay:

LAVARCAM'S COMPLAINT FOR THE SONS OF USNA.

1.

A long shame to my cheek
Is to-night's foul deed in Eman;
The shame of to-night shall sunder
The friendship of many friends.

2.

None goodlier the earth's green breast
E'er nursed than the Sons of Usna;
To see them slain for a woman
Is death of joy to my heart.

3.

Ardàn of the blackbird's voice,
And Ainli, Stag of the Mountain,
And Naisi, King of the Battle,
Their loss is death to my heart.

Then cried she: 'Bar the doors, and shut the windows fast,
Set a good guard, and keep your weapons by your sides!
If they dare set on you, I know what bravery
Is in you. On your heads may victory sit, and good
Go with you where ye go! Fight well, and Fergus' sons
Fight well in your defence!' And, weeping sore, she kissed
And bade them all farewell, then slowly sought the King.

'Now, by thy tongue of truth, what news?' cried Conchobar.
'Good news, and bad,' said she. 'How so?' said Conchobar.
'Good, in that now thou hast, back in this realm, the three
Whose forms of manhood tower o'er all the world; the three
Whose spears are thunderbolts, whose brands are flames of war,
Whose feet on battle-fields are like the tempest's feet
Spurning the sea. Have these with thee, and let the world
Come with its five great fifths against thee, they shall be
Like timorous flocks of birds, like starlings that a shout
Scares from the stubble. Boys they went from us, and men,
Mighty men, come they back. The youngest of the three
In strength is greater now than the eldest that we knew:
And that is my best news. The worst I have in store
Is that the form thy bride took with her when she went
Is not upon her now. Ochone for my poor child!
You have had great hardship since, great hardship must you have had,
To come this changeling back! For every year, three years
Have laid their age on her: the light quencht in her eyes,
The bloom flown from her face; the withering of her flesh
Leaves her an autumn leaf, a sorrow, a thing unknown!'

Thus with her crafty words she lulled the jealous worm
Stinging the King to rage. He quaffed without a word
Cup after cup, brooding. Half he believed her, half
He feared her guile. 'This hag,' thought he, 'winked at her flight,

And now may lie like truth.'   Aloud he said : 'Who now
Will go a second time, and tell me in what shape
Comes Deirdrè back ? '   And thrice he asked ; but no one spoke,
For all men feared to bring some evil on the Land.

Now there was one who sat at meat with him that night,
A stranger in the House of Conchobar, his name
Tren-dorn ; to whom the King, taunting him, cried : ' Tren-dorn,
Haply thy manhood keeps no memory of a wrong
Done to thy youth—or else thou shouldst but little love
The Sons of Usna.   Ay, surely thou hast forgot
Who slew thy father, man ? '   Thereat the man grew red,
Then suddenly pale, and took from next his heart a cloth
Stained with dark blood ; and cried in a wild voice : ' This blood
I bear about me keeps that memory fresher here
That its own colour, King !   This is my father's blood,
By Naisi shed.'   ' Up then,' said Conchobar, ' and see
If Deirdrè's beauty keep as freshly as thy wrong.
Thou wilt not lie to me to-night, if she be fair.'

Then went Tren-dorn, and came to the House of the Red Branch ;
But when he found the doors and windows barred, came fear
Upon him, nor he durst, for aught the King might give,
Demand an entrance there.   ' There is no way,' said he,
' By which a man may come within the hall, and live :
Wrath is upon the Sons of Usna.'   Lingering there
Around the House, whose gloom frowned on him dauntingly,
With feet between two fears driven in two ways, he found
A window, left unbarred for air, whereto he climbed,
And peered within, and saw Deirdrè.   But when he saw her,
As great as was his fear, yet greater was the charm
And witchery of her face : it held him in amaze,
Till, with a sense of eyes upon her, she looked up,

And saw him.   Naisi's foot she pressed and made him see
Eyes at the loop.   He snatched a dead-man from the board,
And flung it with a cast so swift, an aim so true
It struck Tren-dorn ; and stunned, one peering eye dasht out,
He dropped, and, mad with pain, yelled like a dog that feels
His master's lash ; and so went back to Conchobar,
In rage and shame, one eye blind in his bleeding face.

'This is my wage,' he cried, ' got in thy service, King ! '
And many standing by mocked him.   But Conchobar
Frowned on them, and replied : ' This have they done to me.
Take comfort, for that shame great eric shalt thou have.'

' But Deirdre ? Hast thou seen ? How looks she?' And Tren-dorn
Answered : 'To see her face is worth an eye.   This world
Holds no such beauty, King, 'twixt sea and sea, as now
Shines on her.   Blight of age durst never steal its bloom ;
All women else are hags.   Leave her in Naisi's arms,
And he is King of the world, as sure he deems himself,
Barring her in thy house, where now he sits at ease.'

Then Conchobar arose in wrath and jealousy,
Crying : ' Ye see what shame the Sons of Usna heap
Upon me now, shaming the messenger I send,
Even while they feast in my house, even while they keep my Queen,
Barring the doors against me.   Up, for they come in war,
Not peace, to mock my beard with scorning of their King ! '

So, followed by the strength of all his men-at-arms,
He marched upon the House ; and there they made three bands
And circled it about, and gave three mighty shouts
Of war around it, while with flaming brands they came,
And menace of assault.   Then cried Illàn the Fair :
'What men are ye, and wherefore come ye against this House ?'

They answered : 'Conchobar and Ulla ! '   'False the tongue
That slanders those proud names ! ' cried he, 'Against you stands
The surety Fergus gave.'   'Well the young cockerel crows,'
Said Conchobar.   'But shame sits on your brows this night,
Keeping my wife with you ; and save you bring her forth,
Great, by my troth, shall be the vengeance ye shall meet ! '

When Deirdrè heard the voice of Conchobar, the heart
Grew sick within her breast, like a hidden bird that hears
The kestrel cry.   'The pledge of Fergus is no pledge—
We are betrayed ! ' she said.   'Trust but your own good swords,
Forlorn are Usna's Sons ! '   But Naisi frowning said :
'Till it be broke I hold the pledge of Fergus good,
Play on ! '   But Deirdrè knelt, weeping, by Gaier's bed,
And played no more.   Then spake Buiné the Red : 'Take heart !
Let Conchobar be false, but by my head, no shame
Of treachery rests on us ; ' and forth he ran, with all
His warmen after him ; for upon Eman's plain
The best men of his clan had met them as they came,
To be their body-guard.   He rushed around the House,
And slew in that one rush three fifties, and put out
The fires, and trampled all the torches under foot.

And straight at Conchobar he made.   Then cried the King :
'What man art thou, who mak'st such mischief in my ranks ? '
'Buiné the Red,' said he.   Then loud laughed Conchobar :
'Mad son of a mad sire !   Wilt thou be rich by me ? '
'What riches should I have from thee ? '   'Broad lands and good :
A cantred of the lands of Usna's traitor Sons.'
'A good first word,' said he.   'Thereafter ? '   'And withal
My private ear in council—turn but away thy sword ! '
'My sword is turned,' said he.   And so in perjury,
And bribed by Conchobar, he drew his band away

But that same night fell storm on the plough-lands of the bribe,
And a lake rose in wrath, because of that foul wrong
To Usna's Sons ; leaving its bed among the hills
It made those lands a marsh, desolate even to this day,
Well-named even to this day : '*The Marsh of Buiné's Breach.*'

Now Naisi played at chess with Ainli in the hall,
Heeding no whit the noise of strife on Eman's Green.
But when that paused, while spake red Buiné with the King,
Deirdrè cried out : 'O Sons of Usna ! It was truth
I spake to heedless ears : now is my dream come true.
This moment Buiné sells your heads to Conchobar.
By Fergus we are lost, the son false as the sire ! '

' By the red pulse of my heart ! ' said Illàn, ' while this hilt
Is friendly to my hand, though Fergus and his clan
Should leave you, yet will I myself fight to the death,
And never leave you.' Then, his warmen at his back,
Shouting he rushed upon the Ulstermen, and thrice
Circled the Red Branch House, and slew in those three rounds
Three fifties and three more ; leaving upon the Green
Three hundred of the best that stood by Conchobar,
Strong men, before that rush ; and back unhurt he came
To the great hall, where still Naisi with Ainli played.

There for a while he breathed, and drank a mighty draught,
And snatching up a torch out of a sconce, he stood
In the great door, and sent a challenge to the host
Of Conchobar : ' Who dares, let him stand, man to man,
Against me in fair fight ; and vows be laid upon us
To fight unto the death, none aiding. Let him come
With casting-spear, and sword, and thrusting-spear ! 'Tis I,
Illàn the Fair, the Son of Fergus. Come who dares,
Be it my brother, here no kinship let him claim ! '

' By my sword,' said Conchobar, ' the brood of Fergus cast
A shame on me this night !   Come here, Fiachra, my son !
This loud-tongued youth and thou are of one age : two cubs
Whelped in one hour.   He wears his father's arms, go thou
And meet him in mine own.'   Then Fiachra took the arms
Of Conchobar.   ' Fight well, my son, for me this night ! '
His father said, and kissed Fiachra, and sent him forth.

So Fiachra came where stood Illàn, who cried to him :
' What man art thou who comest against me in those arms ? '
' One thou knowest well,' said he, ' the son of Conchobar,
Fiachra the Fair, thy friend.'   ' In a bad cause, O Fiachra !
Comest thou in his arms against me,' said Illàn.
' Be that as it may,' said he, ' I am here to fight with thee.'
' What is thy first weapon ? '   ' The casting-spear.'   ' Come, then,
I am ready,' said Illàn, ' with that let us begin.
Yon moon will be the torch of valour for us both.'

They flung their arms about each other's necks and kissed.
Then was there fought between them a battle fierce and long,
The like whereof was ne'er beheld on Eman's Green,
Till that same night.   And first, like hill-cats lithe and swift
They played with circling feints, to gain some vantage-ground,
Ere darted from their gripe the spears.   Their singing spears
Flew from their hands through the air, like dragons of the air;
Swifter than swallow's flight over the sea.   More swift
Than swallow's veering flight in the air, upon the Green
The Champions raced and veered, subtler than doubling hares.

But good as was their casting, better was their defence ;
For either would they turn the strokes upon their shields,
Or leap aside, or catch the eager-screaming spears
In their strong hands, and hurl them, screaming like falcons, back.

Then cried Illàn the Fair : ' Enough of fair-day sport :
Hast thou no weapon else ? ' Said Fiachra : ' What thou wilt—
Spoil-winner snuffs the field.' ' Fair welcome,' said Illàn,
' To him and thee ! ' They took their thrusting-spears, and each
Drove at the other. Fierce the fight grew, and the grass
Was trampled where they met with fence and thrust, their shields
Took many a dint and gash. At the third interchange
Spoil-winner through the shield of Fergus drove, and tore
Illàn's flesh from his ribs nearest the heart. Thereon
Young Fiachra, with a shout of : ' Conchobar a-boo ! '
Pressed on him. He gave ground. But Deirdrè, who looked forth,
Viewing the battle, cried a wild and woeful cry :
' Think of me, Son of Fergus ! Fight for my sake this night ! '

Then taller grew the Son of Fergus at her cry,
And twice more strong, such rage of battle Deirdrè's voice
Put in her champion. ' Swords ! ' he cried to Fiachra, ' Swords !
End we this battle ! ' Fierce he drove at Fiachra, fierce
He hewed at him, till back he forced him, foot by foot,
Toward where the Red Branch House rose huge, darkening the moon.
But the great roaring shield of Conchobar kept still
His son from hurt ; but now so near his danger drew
It roared loud as the seas in tempest, and its voice
Was answered on the coasts of Ireland by the voice
Of the three magic waves, the wave of Toth, the wave
Of Cleena, and the wave of Rury, roaring loud.

Now that same night within Dunseverick by the sea,
Lay Conall Carnach, Son of Amergin, and heard
The wave of Rury roar, and thought : ' This roaring bodes
Danger to Conchobar.' In haste he took his arms,
Leaped on his fleetest horse and came to Eman Green.

There on the Green he found hosts in array, and men
Dead on the Green, and two in combat by the House
Of the Red Branch—and one was down upon his knee;
For Fiachra then had ta'en a sword-wound in his thigh,
And over him was spread the shield of Conchobar,
Roaring under the moon.   But no man of the host
Durst rescue him, because the vow was on them all.

He spurred amain, and drove, heedless of Deirdrè's shriek,
His blade through Illàn's back, driving it through and through
The basket of his breast.   'Who strikes this coward's blow
To my wounding?' said Illàn.   'I, Conall.   Who art thou?'
'Illàn the Fair, the Son of Fergus,' said the youth,
'An ill deed hast thou done, slaying me; for I guard
The Sons of Usna here.'   Then Conall Carnach sprang
In anguish from his horse.   'Is that the truth?' said he.
'A bad truth!' said Illàn, and like a strake of corn
Caught in the reaper's hand, when the sharp sickle quells
The stiffness of the stalk, drooped his fair head.   No strength
Was left in him to hold a weapon more, and faint
He sank in Conall's arms; and Conall laid him down
Gently upon the grass.   Then terribly he grasped
The shield of Conchobar, and tore it from the grip
Of Fiachra as he crouched.   'What man art thou?' said he.
'The Son of Conchobar, Fiachra, and for his sake
I think nigh death.'   'In that thou hast spoken a true word,'
Said Conall.   'Conchobar shall never take thee now
Alive out of my hands.'   And at a blow he smote
His fair head from his trunk, and dead he left him there.

Then from the ground groaned out Illàn : 'The hand of death
Lies heavily on me now.   If thou be pitiful
Help me into the House, my arms upon me.'   And slow
They came to the great door.   'Set me beside the post,'

Said the dying man, 'and now leave me in peace, and take
Forgiveness for my death.'   Then Conall Carnach leaped
Upon his horse, and rode in wrath, scattering the hosts,
Speaking no word, away, back to Dunseverick strand.

But on the door-post leaned Illàn, trembling and pale,
And gasped for breath.   Anon with his last strength he flung
His shield into the hall, and tottering in, death-blind,
Fell on the floor, panting : ' I am slain in your defence ;
Do valiantly for yourselves.'   And all the floor was red
From the rivers of his veins ; with every word he spoke
More blood came through the lips than breath.   Then Naisi cast
The board away, crying : ' Thou art the pick of three,
And thou hast done the work of three for us this night.
A champion's praise be thine ; for better none could do.'

They raised him in their arms, and Deirdrè o'er him bent.
' Faithful and true thou art, faithful and true ! ' she said,
Weeping ; and on his face, damp with the dews of death,
Rained her hot tears.   She knelt, and with her warm soft mouth
Kissed his cold brow.   Thereat with wistful glazing eyes
He stared on her.   No speech was left him ; but he smiled,
And dead they laid him down, that smile on his dead lips.

Conchobar, when he knew Fiachra lay slain, sent forth
His herald to bring back the body, with his arms ;
And there he made great moan for his dead son, and said :
' I have lost a precious thing, losing thee so, my son !
My valour's flame wast thou, my shield in war, the hope
Of morning to mine eyes ; and now thou art gone from me,
Lost for a toy, a gawd, a woman's face !   O, now
Would I had thee once more, and Deirdrè in her grave ! '
And, arming straight, he came in rage against the House.

Then ran the Ulster men with firebrands round the House
To burn it, with loud shouts of : ' Conchobar a-boo ! '
But valiantly Ardàn rushed on them, and hurled back
The press, and trampled out the fire, and with his men
Slew them in heaps : and so the first watch of the night
He kept the place.   The like did Ainli after him,
Rushing among the hosts of Conchobar, he seemed
A wolf among the flocks ; through them, and under them,
And over them he went : and so he held the place
The second watch of the night.   Last went forth Naisi, and he
Raged like a furious elk among the hounds, and made
The Green of Eman red with slaughtering of the clans
Led on by Conchobar.   And Conchobar himself
With his blade's flat he smote, and brought him to his knee
Beneath his roaring shield.   Then to the Red Branch House
He came victorious back.   So the third watch of the night
He held the place ; and none durst come against it more.

By this the moon had set, the stars young in the sky
Like torches quencht by the sun were paling ; and like stars
Paled by the dawn the torches flickered in the hall,
As Deirdrè in the door, with Gaier in her arms,
Met Naisi with her smile.   Like a dawn-wakened bird,
The boy sang in her arms, for life's mere joy, and laughed
To greet his father.   Tears shone soft in Deirdrè's eyes,
Even as she smiled, and fond the welcome was, she gave
Her champion come once more with victory back to her.

' O, bravely have you done this night ! ' she cried, ' thyself,
And Ainli, and Ardàn.   Said I not well to thee :
' Beware of Conchobar ?   But never could I know,
No, not even I could know, such valour and such might
Was in you as this night ye have put forth for me.
Ye have abasht the world with valour ! '   ' Ah, my girl ! '

Said Naisi, as from her arms he took the boy, 'this might
Thy beauty and thy love put in our hearts.   For thee,
And for this boy, we fought.'   'But now,' she said, 'be ruled
This once by me.   While now their army stands aloof
Let us go forth and seek Dundalgan by the sea,
And there find with Cuchullin rest from Conchobar.'

'Even my own thought,' said he.   And with their linkèd shields
They fenced the women well, and marched in the pale dawn
Forth on the Green ; and all the men of Ulster stood
Half-dazed and slaughter-sick, and little was their will
To stay their going.   Then came Conchobar where stood
Cathvah the Druid.   'See, Cathvah,' said Conchobar,
'Where Naisi goes, and now will he go safe, and rend
The Kingdom with new wars.   Stay him with wizardry,
Or endless wreck will waste the Province we have made.'

Said Cathvah : 'With what vow, if on them I should lay
Druidry, wilt thou bind thy Kingship that no hurt
Shall come upon their lives ? '   'This vow,' said Conchobar,
'On the honour of a King, I ask but for my wife
Whom they have stol'n from me.   Curse me, and curse this land,
If, Deirdrè in my arms, I do them any hurt.'

Then Cathvah on the Green kindled a Druid's fire,
And in the fire he cast magical herbs, that made
A smoke about the feet of Usna's Sons ; and soon
The smoke about their feet spread like a sea, wherein
They seemed to wade in waves ; and, struggling to uplift
Deirdrè above the waves, they battled on, to reach
The shore of their own isle in Alba, where it seemed
Before them full in view.   But Deirdrè cried to them :
'On, on ! ~ This is no sea, cast not your arms away,
To save me !   Cathvah weaves this Druid spell, and winds

The going of our feet with treachery.'   But her words
Went idly by their ears ; for all their sense was dazed
With druidry.   Madly they cast away their spears,
Their shields, and stretched their arms upon the druid smoke
Feebly, to swim upon it ; and staggered to and fro,
Beaten by its waves ; and soon with all their folk they lay
In heaps upon the sward, drowned in that druid sea.

And Deirdrè lay and wept on Naisi's arm, that strove
To save her to the last.   Then came the Ulstermen,
At Conchobar's command, and bound them where they lay.
And so were Usna's Sons by treachery taken there.

THE EIGHTH DUAN.

THE DEATH OF THE SONS OF USNA.

In the first silver light of the young day they brought
The Sons of Usna, bound, to Conchobar ; and there
The cloud of druidry fell from them, and they saw
In anguish and deep rage the cunning net wherein
They had foredone themselves.   But Deirdrè came unbound,
With Gaier in her arms, guarded ; the King's fierce eyes
Flamed on her as she stood, tearless and stern, despair
Clutching her throat, but pride upon her scornful face.

Dumb before Conchobar she stood, never more fair,
Never more proud.   She looked at Naisi ; and such love
Shone in her faithful eyes, that love and jealousy
Tore the King's heart in his breast.   She looked at Conchobar
With such a fearless hate, that madness in his brain

Wrought murderously. 'What peace or comfort shall I have,
Though I have her,' he thought, 'If still her lover live?'
And Deirdrè's face was flame within him, and burnt up
The memory of his vow to Cathvah, and all ruth
Went with his honour; rage seemed weak to glut revenge.

'Have I no friends,' he cried, 'to wreak upon these thieves—
These traitors, my great wrong, slaying them for me now?'
But not a man of all the Province spoke nor moved
To do his bidding. Then, like one wounded, he groaned:
'Have I no friend?' and looked on Eoghan of Fern-moy,
The Son of Durthach, come to make a pact with him,
And craving subsidy. He faltered forth: 'O King,
If there be found none else to serve thee, that will I;
Although to slay men bound be hateful to my hand!'

Then came Maini the Red, son of a Norway King,
To Conchobar, and said: 'O King, this right is mine!
By me their heads shall fall; for these three slew my sire,
And my two brothers. Them I avenge, avenging thee.'

And Deirdrè shrieked like one hurt with a stabbing sword,
And round their necks she flung her beautiful white arms,
And kissed them one by one, piteously through her tears
Murmuring soft words of love. Gaier in childish fear
Wept at her weeping. 'Ah, my girl!' said Naisi, 'right,
Right was thy word, and true, as thy true heart. For sure
Never such treachery stained an Irish King before.
I am happier to lie down in my cold bed, than he
To send me there, and live, and be the thing he is.
Ah Deirdrè! we have lived, now must we die. Farewell!
Pulse of my heart, farewell! Courage, and save the boy.'

From her last clinging kiss then was she torn away
By Eoghan, who drew nigh with Maini, aiding him.
And Maini said: 'The blood of my father, slain by you,
Calls me to shed your blood, or Conchobar might wait
Until his cairn was green, ere I had done this deed.'
'Thou art in thy right,' they said, 'and we bound in thy hand;
But in fair fight we slew thy brothers and thy sire.'

Now a contention rose between the brothers three,
Which of them first should die.   'The youngest,' said Ardàn,
'And that am I.'   'Not so,' said Ainli, 'spare mine eyes
The sorrow of thy death.'   Said Naisi: 'Take my sword,
That sword which Manannàn, the Son of Lir, gave once
To Usna: it shall have the slaying of his Sons;
For with it thou mayest smite our three heads at a blow.'

Shrill as a Banshee shrieked the sword at Naisi's thigh,
As Maini loosed the belt, and took it.   'Put it now,'
Said Naisi, 'to my lips.'   He kissed the sword, and said:
'A good friend thou hast been, and trusty.   Thou hast kept
My life a thousand times; now shalt thou give me death,
And swiftly.'   Then he said to Maini: 'Loose our bonds,
For shame it is to slay men bound.'   Their bonds he loosed,
And in their arms awhile they held each other fast,
And tenderly they took their last farewell, and all
The men of Ulster wept, so piteous was the sight.

There on the sward they knelt, and bared their necks, and twined
Their battle-winning arms around each-other; and so
Knelt Naisi in the midst, and Ainli on his right,
And on his left Ardàn; and high they raised their heads
To look upon the sun, bringing their day of death
In splendour from the east.   And dewy was the morn,
And loudly sang the lark.   Thus they abode the stroke.

Now Maini drew the sword ; and with a second shriek
It flashed out of the sheath. ' Well mayst thou shriek, old friend,'
Said Naisi. ' By my troth, when we spared Conchobar,
That was our fault ! And now, farewell, land of my heart,
Farewell Ireland ! There swims no better land this day
On the waters of the world, with truer comrades in it,
Or wives more loving, fair, and faithful, as I know.
There is no better land, for valour and kindly mirth ;
No better land for harps, music, and sweet-voiced songs
That gush like silver streams of living water through it ;
No better land for love and beauty, and the taste
Of the sweet air of the morn, with horses and with hounds.
O, for the balmy woods of Ireland, for the trees
Of her green woods, the stags of her wild mountain glens !
The fern, the furze, the heath ; the cunning creatures in them,
The shy otter, the stoat, the badger, and the hare !
O, for the swans of her loughs, the salmon of her streams !
O, for the blackbird's note, and the thrush's in the morn,
The cuckoo's coo of spring, the robin's autumn dirge !
All these, I loved them well, and Ireland has my love ;
Would that we died for her ! Maini, thy hand be true ;
And when we three are dead, I charge thee, give my sword
To the hand of Manannàn. Now, courage, man, and strike ! '

Then, for the last time shrieked the sword, and with that shriek
Together on the sward fell their three heads : the sod
Of Ireland drank their blood. None better ever dimmed
The dew on the shamrock leaves, or turned the daisy's face
Red on the Irish sod. So died, slain at one blow,
In their fresh prime of life, Usna's three noble Sons.

Deirdrè, meanwhile, the guards led back to the Red Branch House,
And as she went she heard the three marvellous cries
The sword of Manannàn sent forth, and at the third

She felt the cold of death clutching her heart; and three
Great drops of blood were shed from the breast above her heart;
And so she knew their death, yet kept for Gaier's sake,
The sick faint from her brain; and in the Red-Branch House
Sat down without a tear, lulling him in her arms.

There she began to chant a Sleep-song, sweet and low,
Crooning the pain from her heart in sweet music, so sweet,
It seemed as though the Swans of Lir were singing there
Low dirges of the sea.   And Gaier slept; and all
Who heard that music slept, for the magical sweet pain
That seized their dreaming souls.   And Deirdrè, singing still,
With Gaier in her arms, walked out upon the Green,
And no man stayed her steps; whither she would she went.

And fair and terrible she looked that morn.   She seemed
A phantom of the morn, as on swiftly she strode,
Singing, over the Green, with feet that trembled not
Nor stayed; o'er gory heaps of dead men, slain for her—
Her own blood on her breast, their blood upon her feet
And on her sweeping skirts.   The dead appalled her not—
She saw them not, but still fled from the living eye,
To the hills away.   From far she saw where on the plain
They dug in the green grass three black-mouthed graves.   She saw,
And shed no tear; but on she hastened by the way
Towards Dundalgan, on, with Gaier in her arms.

Far, on Dundalgan's shore, Cuchullin heard the wave
Of Rury roar amain, as Naisi on the Green
Smote down the King; and now, furiously driving, bound
To Eman in his car, he came.   Swiftly the steeds
Leaped at the voice of Laeg, his charioteer, the Son
Of Riangowra, high the wheels bounded at every stride;
And in his battle-car the Champion stood, full-armed.

There in his path he saw a woman, holding high
A child, stand, with a cry: 'Stay! stay, Cuchullin, stay!'
And pale she looked and wild, and on her tunic's breast
Three gouts of blood, and blood upon her skirts and feet:
And that was Deirdrè.   There he stayed the car, and down
He leaped to her ; and she stared on him, crying : 'Swift help
Thou bringest Conchobar ; but he is safe, and there
Lies Naisi slain, there lie the Sons of Usna slain!'   .

'How should this fall!' he groaned.   'And Fergus, where is he ?
Is he too slain with them?'   'Nay, nay,' said she, 'he feasts
With Barach, who hath laid, at Conchobar's command,
His champion's vow upon him : *Ne'er to refuse a feast.*
Illàn is slain for us, but Buiné sold our heads,
For broad lands, to the King.'   And Deirdrè made this lay :

DEIRDRÈ'S SONG OF THE TREACHEROUS FEAST.

1.

A song for thee, O Champion!
A song of the traitor's guile :
The foxes have slain the lions,
The crows have harried the eagles.

2.

A feast, a feast in the North,
And Barach made that feast:
There, breaking a vow for a vow,
Fergus the Feaster sits.

3.

But Usna's Sons lie slain
In Eman of the spears :
They tamed the spears with their valour,
But treachery's nets o'erthrew them.

4.
Thrice shrieked the sword of their slaying
The sword of their safety slew them :
The foxes have slain the lions,
The crows have harried the eagles.

'Ochone!' Cuchullin said.   'A black day is this day
For the Red-Branch!   This deed of Conchobar's has brought
Sorrow and shame on us, and henceforth sorrow and shame
Will wake us in the morn, and in the night lie down
Beside us where we lie !   But who gave them their death ?'

'Maini the Red,' said she.   'By him fell their three heads.'
'Not long then, by my sword, shall Maini wear his head
Upon him, for this deed,' said he ;   'and were they slain
Under my surety, well must Conchobar himself
Look to his life to guard it.'   'Would it were thou indeed,'
Said she, 'that brought us back ; for now well had we sped.
Surely one foolish hour has brought long days of woe.

'But yesternight they lived, their help in their own hands,
Now is the day but young, and yet they live no more
For any help of thine.   But here, upon thy vow
To succour those who need, I charge thee, take this child,
Naisi's and mine ; bring him to the Isle of Manannàn,
There shalt thou leave him safe with the Wizard of the Sea,
To foster him, and rear a champion of the blood
Of Usna, to avenge the wrongs his father had.'

'This will I do,' said he.   And so into his arms
She gave her son.   Then first, kissing the sleeping child,
The rivers of her tears thawed in her eyes ; and long
She bent o'er him and wept, sighing : 'My boy, my boy !'

'Farewell!' she said, 'With thee goes the best blood of my heart,
And with thee goes the warmth out of my breast! Sound, sound
Thy sleep be; but the sleep that holds thy father's eyes
Be far from thine! Farewell, for of the dead am I,
And to the dead go back!' Then, with heartbreaking sobs
Choked in her breast, she turned, and to Cuchullin waved
A last farewell. The tears were warm in his blue eyes,
Mounting his car again with Gaier in his arms,
Tenderly held. And slow the car passed from her sight.

There for a little space on the thymy sward she lay,
Nigh death for sobbing, cold, weeping away her blood
In tears of agony. A robin from a thorn
Burst into gurgling song, for joy of the glad sun:
She felt it like the pain of wakening life in one
Snatched from the sea, rose up, and like a homeless wraith
Drawn by the spells of death from the sweet world of day
Back to the grave, she fled back to her place of dole.

To the three graves she came—three shallow pits, lined all
With slabs rough-hewn, and set anglewise like three rays
Of one black flower of death. And stones unhewn they brought
To build the chambers three, ere over them they heaped
One common cairn. And there, a stone-cast off, were laid
On hurdles, side by side, the three brothers. And there
On pillows of green sods, each in its proper place,
With eyes closed as in sleep were laid their three pale heads.

When Deirdrè saw that sight, she tore her sunny hair,
And beat her breast. 'Ochone that ever we came here!
A great sin, O sweet Sons of Usna, did ye sin
Against yourselves, to sail from Alba of the Lakes,
Against my counsel! O, for Alba, of the deer!
Would ye were hunting now in Alba, and myself
To keep your house for you!' And there made she this lay :

DEIRDRÈ'S LITTLE LAMENTATION FOR THE
SONS OF USNA.

1.

O, pleasant, pleasant my life was
In Alba of the Mountains,
Contention was none between us,
Myself and thee, O Naisi!

2.

But once, once, in thy lightness
Thou slewest my sleep with sorrow,
When, victory on thy banners,
Thou camest from Inverness.

3.

A hidden kiss was my wronging,
My bale was Duntroon's brown daughter:
To her thou gavest, O Naisi!
A kiss in my despite.

4.

A milk-white doe did he send her,
The messenger of his wooing,
A bright-eyed elf of the forest,
Beside her a frisking fawn.

5.

The tale was gall to my gladness,
And fire in the jealous woman:
I launched my skiff on the waters,
And the port of my dream was death.

6.

Ah, why did ye save your slayer,
Ardàn and Ainli, my brothers!
They loosed my tears with their kindness,
They quenched the fire of my heart.

7.

Thrice Naisi swore by his valour,
He took his arms for a witness,
That nevermore would he grieve me
Till he joined the hosts of the dead.

8.

Ah ! were she here whom I hated,
And saw him low where he lieth,
Two friends in grief would we wail him,
Her tears would answer my tears.

9.

But now alone in my sorrow
No woman weeps with my weeping,
None raises the keene beside me,
None lifts the weight of my heart !

With a low moan, stumbling, she groped for Naisi's breast,
Like a faithful dog that creeps to die by his dead lord,
And there lay like one dead.　And no man of the guard
Durst speak to her a word, for pity, and the awe
Of her terrible white face ; but news to Conchobar
Was brought, that she was there, lying among the dead.

Thereat the King rejoiced with a grim joy ; for fierce
Had been his rage that none could find her, nor could tell
The manner of her flight from the House of the Red-Branch.
And straight he gave command to bury the three Sons
Of Usna, and to bring Deirdrè before his face.

But when they came to lay the brothers in their tomb,
She was a thing distraught.　She kissed them o'er and o'er,
Going, like a beast of chase that fondles her dead cubs
Full in the hunter's eye, restlessly to and fro
From bier to bier, tearless, low-moaning.　Naisi first,

And Naisi last, she kissed passionately, till her lips
Were dabbled with his blood.   At last she rose, and stood
Over them, her great eyes glaring from her white face,
Blood on her piteous lips, blood on her draggled hair,
Blood on her silken robe ; yet in her beauty still
Superb and terrible.   With such a majesty
Of woe might come once more out of the dreadful past
Some warrior queen, death-pale, risen from some last lost field
Of slaughter, all bestrained with Ireland's dearest blood,
To warn her of new woes.   So Deirdrè looked that day
When she stood up to raise her keene over the Sons
Of Usna : and she sang this death-song by their tomb :

DEIRDRÈ'S LAMENTATION FOR THE SONS OF USNA.

THE FIRST SORROW.

1.

The daughters of beauty weep
In the desolate halls of Eri,
Hushed are the sons of music
In the lonely House of Kings !

2.

Long to me is the day
Without the Three, without the Three,
Three lions of war, three dragons,
Three sons of a noble King.

3.

They were great of heart, they were comely
Beyond the champions of Eri :
Forlorn is the House of Usna,
Broken the great Red-Branch.

4.

Ah! why, why have ye left me
Ye beautiful Sons of Usna?
Would I had gone to my slaughter
Ere ye were slain for my sake!

THE BEATING OF THE BREAST.

Ochone, ochone-a-rie!
They are gone, they have left me lonely!
Ochone-a-rie!   Ochone
For the hearts that beat no more!

THE SECOND SORROW.

1.

Long to me is the day
Without the Three, without the Three;
In onset dreadful as thunder,
But gentle to me their love.

2.

Like the sister strings of a harp,
They made sweet music together;
And I the fourth in their chiming,
Our hearts were sweet strings in tune.

3.

When flamed your swords o'er the battle
Great Kings were abasht before you;
But sweet to me were your faces,
Like honey your words of love.

4.

Ah! why, why did you leave me,
Ye beautiful Sons of Usna?
Would I had gone to my slaughter
Ere ye were slain for my sake!

THE RENDING OF THE HAIR.

Ochone! Ochone-a-rie!
My head is shorn of its beauty
Ochone-a-rie!   Ochone
For the mighty that wake no more.

THE GREAT LAMENTATION.

1.

Ochone for the land left lonely,
Without the Three, without the Three!
The warmth of the sun goes with you
To the cold house of the dead !

2.

Without them the Red-Branch House
Is a place of ghosts, of black horror;
The feasts of the mighty mourn them,
The women of Eri weep !

3.

My curse on Fergus, that left them,
My curse on Buiné, that sold them,
My curse on Cathvah, that bound them,
My curse on Maini, that slew them !

4.

And my curse's curse on the King
That snared them with words of honey,
Black hills of hate be above him,
My curse upon Conchobar !

5.

O better than mother's love
Were Naisi's arms around me !
O gentler than loving brothers
Were Ainli and Ardàn !

6.

They fed me with love, they kept me
With spoil in their nest of eagles ;
Without them the fields of Eri
Are blasted, and black the skies !

7.

Ochone for the Land left lonely
Without the Three, without the Three !
The warmth of the sun goes with you
To the cold house of the dead !

THE CLOSING OF THE TOMB.

In the house without a fire
Heap the black stones over me ;
With Naisi where cold he lies
Let the clods cover me !

And when they laid the Sons of Usna in their tomb
Deirdrè would have lain down with Naisi, and endured
With him the covering stones ; but the guards forced her thence,
In pity pitiless ; and so to Conchobar
Was she brought back, more like a corpse dug from the grave
Than a living woman, fair, with red blood in her veins.

THE NINTH DUAN.

THE DEATH OF DEIRDRÈ.

Now Fergus, when the feast was done, sped from the North,
In a vague fear, and found the Sons of Usna dead,
And Illàn dead, and Buiné perjured and sold—a thing
Of common scorn.   And rage came on him as a storm

Blowing a fire in the furze : and gathering all his clan,
With many a chief of name, he wasted the fair fields
Of Eman, and burnt down the House of the Red-Branch
And the great Hall of Arms, and laid on Conchobar
Slaughters and shames, and burnt, with fire kindled in dung,
The House of Eman's Kings, over his head.   Then laid
Cathvah his druid curse on the King's homeless head,
And banned out of his line the Kingdom evermore :
So lordship passed away from Eman of the Kings.

But Fergus with his band, when in his fierce revenge
He had left Eman waste : folkless its peopled plains,
Ashes for splendour, brands for rafters, shame for pride,
Passed o'er the northern fords of Shannon, and was great
With Meave and Aillil, made the captain of their hosts
In Olnemacta.   There he dwelt, and year by year
Pressed with implacable war on Conchobar, and rent
The Province in his hand, and took from him the plains
Of Cuilny of the Herds, and ten years long the wars
Between the great Red-Branch led on by Conchobar,
And the wild clans of the West who followed after Meave
And Fergus, with no truce raged on from sea to sea.
And many a noble champion fell, and in those wars
Conchobar took the wound that brought him to his death.

But over the three graves of Usna's Sons they heaped
One mighty mound, and long the Men of Ulla mourned
The day that saw their death.   ' That was the day,' men said
' Of the rending of the Branch, the sundering of old friends,
When from the home of Kings the splendour passed away !'

And from that day the mind of Conchobar was changed.
Wild were his moods, and dark the passion that belied
The staidness of his youth.   Strange laughter and strange tears
Would shake the gravity and sternness of his mien,

And with a joyless rage, that seemed but as the lash
Of inward torturers, would be, as ne'er before,
Rage after women.   Yet still in council or in war
His manhood shewed no taint, and never seemed he less
Than a great King, with power to bind the wills of men.

But now his majesty shone with a fitful face,
As when, her zenith nigh, haughtily the full moon
Rides on a night of storm, fighting the rack, and clouds
Drive on her in black hosts, and she with splendour tames
Their crests, clothing their gloom in liveries of her light.

A year was Deirdrè held a captive in the house
Of Conchobar ; but small the joy he had of her,
For like a wedded corpse lay she beside the King,
Making his bed a tomb.   Never a smile she gave him
Never a word, but dumb, with the sad eyes of the dead,
She stared his raving dumb, and like an eagle caged
Would crouch the livelong day, yet died not ; for the food
They brought her she would eat.   But sometimes, when the sun
Shone on her hair, too soon grown lustre-sick, her eyes
Would suddenly kindle.   Then from her lorn harp she drew
Soft wailing tones, and oft her Banshee's voice would raise
In broken strains wild songs, bodings of coming war,
Or dirges for the dead.   And so she lived a year.
And in this wise at last her death-day came to her.

It chanced that to the Court of Conchobar was come
Eoghan of Fern-moy, son of Durthach, he who stood
By Maini when he slew Usna's three Sons ; and now
He came to make new pact of friendship with the King.

Then Conchobar began in bitterness of heart
To jest with him, and said : ' I have taken from thy hands
A wanton wife ; but now, for all the pains I have
To make her mirth and glee, I cannot win so much
As one fair smile from her ; nor can with any sport
Or toy that women love, bring to her greensick face
The courage of her youth. Yet hath she sport enough
For any amorous boy she dotes on. Take her thou,
I am sick of her pale face ! Take her, and watch her tame
Or what thou wilt, so I look on her face no more.'

When Eoghan saw Deirdrè, her wonderful wild face
Wrought witchery on him. Still the fading of her prime
Left her the fairest thing for beauty in the world.
And so it was agreed between them she should go
With Eoghan when he went. And thus they went : the car
Of Eoghan first, and he stood in it, like a King ;
The car of Deirdrè next, and she, robed like a Queen,
Sat in it ; and the last the car of Conchobar,
Who brought them on their way, guarding them with his guard.

So rode they by the way to the great fair they held
Upon Murthemny plain, and as they went, they came
To the borders of the realm. There suddenly in her car
Deirdrè rose up, and cast before her a wild look
On Eoghan, then she cast behind her a wild look
On Conchobar. And he jeeringly cried to her :
' Ah, Deirdrè, the shy glance of a ewe between two rams
Thine eyes have cast this day on Eoghan and on me ! '

This taunt, stabbing her brain, stirred in her a swift sense
Of insult and of shame. With a mad laugh she sprang
Sheer from her car, head first, and on the mearing-stones
Dashed out her life. So swift went Deirdrè to her death :
And two-and-twenty years were all the years of her life.

Upon the car they laid the fair load of her corse,
The death-blood in her hair scarce cold, her breast still warm,
Palled like a Queen, over her the royal cloak
Of Conchobar, the cloak of Eoghan under her,
Her youth vexed now no more with weariness of days.

To Eman was she brought. There on the bleak hill-side,
Where first she saw the graves of Usna's Sons, they made
Her grave, and all alone they laid her like a Queen ;
And over her they raised the mighty cairn that looks
Upon the royal cairn of Usna's Sons, and all
The mounds of slaughter heapt on Eman's plain. And there,
On that bleak hill, the tomb of Deirdrè to this day
Sits desolate, in the desolation that she made.

THE LAMENTATION
FOR THE THREE SONS OF TURANN

THE LAMENTATION FOR THE THREE SONS OF TURANN,

WHICH TURANN, THEIR FATHER, MADE OVER THEIR GRAVE.

THE LITTLE LAMENTATION.

1.

Low lie your heads this day,
My sons! my sons!
Make wide the grave, for I hasten
To lie down among my sons.

2.

Bad is life to the father
In the house without a son,
Fallen is the House of Turann,
And with it I lie low.

THE FIRST SORROW.

1.

The staff of my age is broken!
Three pines I reared in Dun-Turann,
Brian, Iuchar, Iucharba,
Three props of my house they were.

2.

They slew a man to their wounding,
In the fierceness of their youth !
For Kian, the son of Caintè,
Their comely heads lie low.

3.

A dreadful deed was your doing,
My sons ! my sons !
No counsel ye took with me
When ye slew the son of Caintè.

4.

A bad war with your hands
Ye made upon Innisfail,
A bad feud on your heads
Ye drew when ye slew no stranger.

5.

And cruel was the blood-fine.
That Lugh of the outstretched arm,
The avenging son of Kian,
Laid on you for his father.

6.

Three apples he claimed, a sow-skin,
A spear, two steeds and a war-car,
Seven swine, and a staghound's whelp,
A spit, three shouts on a mountain.

7.

A little eric it seemed
For the blood of Dè-Danann,
A paltry eric and foolish,
Yet there was death for the three !

THE SECOND SORROW.

1.

Crafty was Lugh, when he laid
That fine on the sons of Turann,
And pale we grew when we fathomed
The mind of the son of Kian.

2.

Three apples of gold ye brought him
From the far Hesperian garden ;
Ye slew the King of Greece
For the skin that heals all wounds.

3.

Ye took from the King of Persia
The spear more deadly than dragons ;
It keeps the world in danger
With the venom of its blade.

4.

Ye won from the King of Sicil
His horses and his war-car,
The fleetness of wings their fleetness,
Their highway the land and the sea.

5.

The King of the Golden Pillars
Yielded the swine to your challenge,
Each night they smoked at the banquet,
Each morning they lived again.

6.

Ye took from the King of Iceland
His hound like the sun for splendour,
Ye won by your hands of valour
Those wonders, and brought them home.

7.

But short was the eric of Lugh
When your hearts grew hungry for Turann ;
For Lugh had laid upon you
Forgetfulness by his craft.

THE GREAT LAMENTATION.

1.

Death to the sons of Turann
Had Lugh in his crafty mind :
' Yet lacks of my lawful eric
The spit, three shouts on the mountain.'

2.

The strength of a babe was left us
At the hearing of that word,
Brian, Iuchar, Iucharba,
Like dead men they fell down.

3.

But Brian your courage kindled,
My sons! my sons!
For the Island of Finchory
A year long they searched the seas.

4.

Then Brian set the clearness
Of crystal upon his forehead,
And, his water-dress around him,
Dived through the waves' green gloom.

5.

Days twice-seven was he treading
The silent gloom of the deep,
His lanterns the silver salmon
To the sea-sunk Isle of Finchory.

6.

Soft shone the moony splendour
Of the magic lamps of Finchory.
There sat in their hall of crystal
The red-haired ocean-wraiths.

7.

Twice-fifty they sat and broidered
With pearls their sea-green mantles;
But Brian strode to their kitchen
And seized a spit from the rack.

8.

Soft rippled their silvery laughter,
Like laughter of summer wavelets :
' Strong is the son of Turann,
But stronger the weakest here.

9.

' And now, should we withstand thee,
No more shouldst thou see thy brothers ;
Yet keep the spit for thy daring,
Brian, we love the bold.'

10.

Then glad ye sailed away,
My sons ! my sons !
To the Hill of Shouts in Lochlànn,
To the Mountain of Miochan.

11.

There met them the friends of Kian,
Sword-mates of the son of Cainte,
Guarding the mount, they stood,
Miochan and his three stout sons.

12.

Oh ! bitter were your battles
In Greece, in Spain, and in Persia,
But bitterer far that fight
On the Mountain of Miochan !

13.

A dead man ye left Miochan,
Thrust through by the spear of Brian,
Dead men ye left his sons,
Corc, Conn, and Oodh, dead men.

14.

But bored were your three fair bodies,
My sons ! my sons !
Bored through by the spears of the sons
Of Miochan of the Mountain.

15.

The sun could shine through their wounds,
The swallows fly through their bodies,
When Brian raised his brothers
To give three shouts on that Mountain.

16.

Ye raised your manly voices,
My sons ! my sons !
More blood came from you than breath
When ye gave your shouts on that Mountain.

17.

Bleeding, down to the ship
Led Brian his bleeding brothers :
' Our lives, with the Skin of Healing,
. Fooled Lugh from our hands ! ' they said.

18.

Then softly in the ship
Laid Brian his fainting brothers ;
By courage he kept his life
To bring them alive to land.

19.

' I see the hills of Dun-Turann,
And Tara of the Kings ! '
Glad and sad were the three
When they saw Ben-Edar above them.

20.

A joyful man was your father,
To greet you living, my sons
A sorrowful man was I
When I saw your deadly wounds.

21.

In Tara of the Kings
I bent before Lugh, I humbled
Before him this hoary head :
' Full eric we bring thee, Lugh ! '

22.

' A great eric, Lugh,
My sons have paid for thy father,
Heal now with the Skin of Healing
The weakness of their wounds ! '

23.

'Bring then thy sons before me!'
Said Lugh; and we came before him:
Two eyes were dry in all Tara
To see them, shrunk with their wounds!

24.

Said Lugh: 'I take from your hands
The eric, ye Sons of Turann;
No bond is on me this day
To yield you the Skin of Healing.'

25.

Then burst o'er Tara's Green
A groan from the hosted kings,
As Brian raised his brothers
To look in the face of Lugh.

26.

Said Brian: 'I slew thy father,
But now I bring thee a blood-fine,
The greatest that man on man
E'er laid since the sun was born.

27.

'I slew thy father: full eric
I bring thee—yet let me die;
But heal with the Skin of Healing
My brothers, to be thy men.'

28.

'Nay,' said Iuchar and Iucharba,
'Our blood be cast in the eric,
The best the sun sees for valour
Is Brian—save him alone!'

29.

'No mercy ye showed my father,'
Said Lugh, 'when his hands of pleading
Ye scorned.   No hurt or no healing
I owe you: your fine is paid.'

30.

Hard-eyed, to the dun of Tara
He turned his feet from your succour.
Ye won him the world's High-Kingship,
He left you with your wounds!

31.

Then faint ye sank by your father,
My sons! my sons!
Said Brian: 'Unjust, O Lugh,
Is the justice of thy craft!

32.

'No wrong like our wrong, O father!
No sorrow like thy sorrow!
We blent no fraud with our valour,
Nor gave him guile for his guile.

33.

'Great were the deeds we did
In Spain, in Greece, and in Persia;
But base and black is the deed
Of Lugh to us three in Tara.'

34.

Ah! pale were your lips that kissed me,
My sons! my sons!
Heart-sick, the three lay down
To die on the Green of Tara.

35.

Dim stared their eyes for the sky,
Their faint hands groped for each other,
Last hope of the House of Turann,
My sons lay down in death.

THE DEATH-SONG OF TURANN.

1.

Low lie your heads this day,
My sons! my sons!
The strong in their pride go by me,
Saying: 'Where are thy sons?'

2.

They spit on my grief, they sully
The snows of my age upon me,
Sonless I stand in Tara,
A laughter, a lonely shame.

3.

How shall I walk in strength
In the gathering of the chiefs ?
A shaking leaf is my valour,
Wanting your spears about me.

4.

How shall I sit in honour
In the counsel of the kings ?
My beard of wisdom the scorner
Shall pluck, with none to defend me.

5.

Happy the dead lie down,
Not knowing the loss of children :
My life in your grave lies dead,
And I go down to my children.

6.

Without you, my hoary age
Is a faltering of the feet.
Without you, my knees that tremble
Go stumbling down to the grave.

7.

Bad is life to the father
In the house without a son,
Fallen is the House of Turann,
And with it I lie low !

NOTES

THE DOOM OF THE CHILDREN OF LIR

P. 3. *The Daghda's dun*. The Daghda was a patriarchal demigod, father of the divine race of De Danann.

P. 4. *Fomorian ships*. The Fomorians were sea-rovers, who for centuries made raids upon the Irish coasts.

P. 11. *Derryvarragh*. A lake in Westmeath; *Sruth-na-Moyle*, the tide-way between Ireland and Scotland; Erris Domnann, possibly Erris Head, in Mayo; *Inis Glory*, an island on the coast of Kerry.

P. 24. *Twixt Erin and Albain*. Ireland and Scotland. *Erin* and *Albain* are genitive cases of *Eri* and *Alba*, frequently used as nominatives, as I have sometimes done, for metrical reasons.

THE FATE OF THE SONS OF USNA

P. 47. *Eman of the Kings*. *Eman Macha*, the seat of the High-Kings of Ulster, was near Armagh (*Ard-Macha*). The Irish names of the Provinces are *Ulla* (Ulster); *Laigen* (Leinster); *Mumha* (Munster); *Connachta*, formerly *Olnemachta* (Connaught).

P. 47. *The cath-barr of a King*. The insignia of an Irish King included the *cath-barr* (helmet) of gold; the *Ard-roth*, or wheel-brooch; and the 'Belt of Royalty.'

P. 47. *A golden Branch of Music*. A peal of small bells, of gold, silver, or bronze, according to his professional rank, and arranged upon a stem or branch, was the distinguishing mark of a Bard. Their sound 'lulled anger to sleep.'

P. 49. *The colours of a King*. The colours distinctive of the different classes of society were regulated by strict sumptuary laws, first formulated by Eochaidh 'of the Clothes.' One colour was prescribed for servants, two for rent-paying farmers, three for officers, five for chiefs, six for *ollavs* (doctors or learned men) and poets, seven for Kings. The King wore the three grave colours of age, symbolic of wisdom, and the four gay colours of youth, symbolic of practical activity.

159

P. 53. *The Hounds of Ulla.* The race of Rury was called the 'Race of Hounds;' hound being a term of honour. *Con* or *Cu*, which means hound, enters into the names of many chiefs, *e.g.* Conchobar (Hound of Glory), Cuchullain (Hound of Culann), &c.

P. 56. *Sovarchy.* The Irish name of the St Johnswort.

P. 57. *Lavarcam, the Conversation-Dame.* This functionary collected · for the King all the gossip and scandal of his court, anticipating the Society newspaper of to-day.

P. 59. *And for his vow he had: Ne'er to refuse a feast.* The Champion's vow was taken when he first received his arms from the King, in token of his championship. However whimsical this vow (*geis*) might be, it was held peculiarly sacred, taking precedence over all other obligations.

P. 72. *The secret message.* This refers to a mode of sending messages in which the meaning was conveyed by the manner in which twigs or rushes were knotted or interwoven.

P. 73. *Their Pot of Avarice.* When a Bard, or company of Bards, visited a King, a vessel called the 'Pot of Avarice' was presented to him, to receive his gifts. If he were generous, they praised him, if stingy, they satirized him; and the Bard's satire had the power of producing sickness, or even death.

P. 78. *Under the dun west-wind.* The Bards gave colours to the winds; to the east wind, crimson; to the south wind, white; to the north wind, black; to the west wind, dun; to the intermediate winds, intermediate colours.

P. 90 *In eric for his death.* The eric was a blood-fine paid to the slain person's kinsfolk or friends in satisfaction for his slaying.

P. 92. *Red-maned Scatha.* This was an Amazon who kept a school of arms for young warriors in the Isle of Skye. Cuchullin and the Sons of Usna were among her pupils.

P. 93. *Their Irish slings.* The staff-sling of the Bardic tales no doubt resembled the sling used by Irish schoolboys in quite recent times. It consisted of a staff of yew, or some other springy wood, to the more flexible upper end of which a thong of leather was attached. The thong was tightened and held in the hand which grasped the lower end of the staff, the staff being thus bent like a bow. The stone was inserted between the upper end of the staff and the leather thong, close to its attachment, and the cast was made by a strong forward stroke of the staff, the stone being released by letting go the unattached end of the thong. The spring of the staff thus added something to the force of the cast.